HOW TO BE A GIRLY GIRL IN JUST TEN DAYS

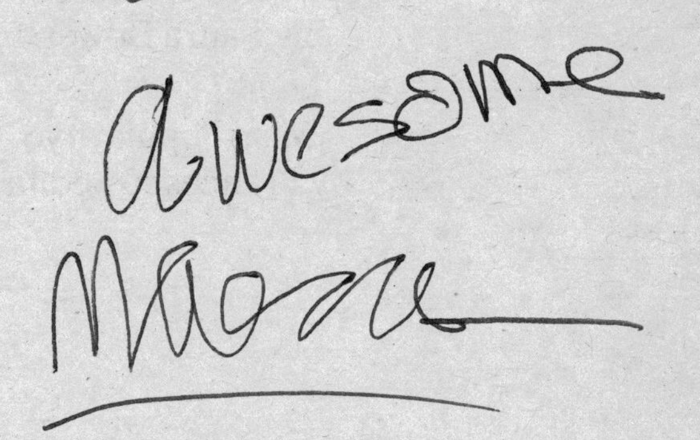

candy apple books...
just for you.
sweet. fresh. fun.
take a bite!

The Accidental Cheerleader
by Mimi McCoy

The Boy Next Door
by Laura Dower

Miss Popularity
by Francesco Sedita

HOW TO BE A GIRLY GIRL IN JUST TEN DAYS

by LISA PAPADEMETRIOU

SCHOLASTIC INC.

New York Toronto London Auckland Sydney
Mexico City New Delhi Hong Kong Buenos Aires

ISBN-13: 978-0-439-89058-8
ISBN-10: 0-439-89058-6

 Published by Scholastic Inc., 557 Broadway, New York, NY 10012.
SCHOLASTIC, CANDY APPLE, and associated logos are trademarks and/or registered trademarks of Scholastic Inc.

12 11 10 9 8 7 6 5 4 8 9 10 11 12/0

Printed in the U.S.A.
First printing, July 2007

This book is dedicated to my kooky and sweet red-haired best friend, Meghan Pappenheim.
— L.P.

DAY ONE

THURSDAY

HOROSCOPE

Aries (March 20–April 21)

That cutie you're crushin' on will be giving mixed signals, but don't give up! It won't take long before you find he's just *so* into you!

"Here's the thing — gingham check is a complete cliché," Lindsay said as she reached over to swipe a couple of French fries from my plate. She ignored me completely as I gave her hand a playful swat, dipping the stolen goods into my pool of ketchup. "I mean, why shouldn't Dorothy wear a red dress, you know? It would go much better with the ruby slippers."

"I think the idea is that she grew up on a farm in Kansas," I ventured.

"Well, right. Okay, so she could be wearing a

potato sack," Lindsay went on. "Or a *flowered* dress." She grabbed another fry, and I let her get away with it. "Or anything — anything but that stupid blue-and-white check! It's been done to death!" She stabbed the air with the fry to make her point.

"Are you sure you want to mess with a classic?" I asked.

"Don't even get me started," Lindsay replied. "You should see what I've got in mind for the flying monkeys."

"I can't wait." This was the truth. Lindsay Sweet is my best friend and has been since before we were born. No, I'm not kidding. Our moms met in Lamaze class, and when they realized that their due dates were a week apart, they decided that we were destined to be best friends forever. Which has turned out to be true, so far, even though Lindsay and I are about as different as two people can get.

For example, Lindsay was wearing red-and-black-striped tights under a pair of cutoff jeans, a black long-sleeved T-shirt under a red short-sleeved concert T-shirt for some band that I'd never heard of, and black Converse low-top sneakers. She had twirled her long curly red hair into a doughnut on each side of her head, Princess Leia–style, and she had on bright red lipstick — the only makeup she ever wears.

I, on the other hand, had on a blue T-shirt and jeans. My hair is brown and cut short around my face. The last time my mom went to see her hairdresser — Jacques — she insisted that I come along "to do something with my hair." Jacques told me that he was going to make me look like "Audrey Hepburn in *Roman Holiday*," and since I had no idea what that meant, I got intimidated and said, "Okay." So then he chopped off all of my hair, and now half the time people mistake me for a boy. Which isn't helped by the fact that everyone calls me "Nick" instead of my real name, which is Nicolette.

When she saw what had happened to my head, Lindsay threw me a little Good-bye-Hair Party. It involved a sympathy card and an ice-cream cake.

Anyway, so Lindsay is really into drama stuff, and she had just signed up to do the costumes and makeup for the school's production of *The Wizard of Oz*.

"People are going to run screaming from the theater at the sight of my flying monkeys," Lindsay said now, reaching for my fruit punch. She had her own food, by the way; she just always seems to prefer mine. I grabbed her chocolate chip cookie in retaliation and broke off half.

"Sounds like a good time," I told her.

"That's showbiz." Her hazel eyes twinkled as she smiled around the straw.

"So, how often do you have to be at rehearsal?" I asked.

"I'll be there, don't worry," she said, reading my mind. "Nobody in the cast and crew wants to miss the big game — we'll *all* be there next Thursday. So you'd better make it worth our while!"

Our basketball team was having an amazing season — so far. But our last game was coming up in a week, and it was against Westlake Middle School, who put a major hurt on us last year. There must be something in the water over in Westlake, because those girls are gigantic. Coach Chin is always telling us to "work our low centers of gravity," which basically means run a lot and steal the ball as much as you can. But it isn't easy when you're going up against people who can cross the entire floor in three easy steps. "We'll do our best," I said with a sigh.

"I don't care about that," she teased. "Just win!" She took another sip from my punch, producing a hollow slurping sound.

"You drank the whole thing!" I cried.

"Sorry." Lindsay winced sheepishly. "I'll get you another."

I rolled my eyes. "I'll do it," I said, swiping the cup. "You'd probably drink the whole thing on the way back to the table."

"Good point," she admitted as she popped a piece of her cookie into her mouth and munched it cheerfully.

I climbed out of my orange plastic seat and crossed to the front of the cafeteria. Lindsay and I always sit in the same spot — far right at the back. As far away from the garbage cans as you can get.

Digging some money out of my pocket, I paid for a refill at the register, then headed over to the drink dispenser and pressed my cup against the metal lip. The machine clanged and ground, then spat ice into my cup. I put the cup under the punch and let the purple liquid fizz down in a stream. I waited for the bubbles to die back, then filled it up to the absolute top. I was just fitting the lid over the cup when I turned —

— and ran into someone's green shirt. Half of the fruit punch soaked him, half splattered the front of my T-shirt.

"Omigosh!" I cried. "Oh, I am so sorry!" Reaching behind me, I grabbed a wad of napkins and pressed them against my victim's shirt.

"That's okay," he said, but just as I pulled away the napkins, I realized that someone had left an open packet of mustard sitting on them . . . bright yellow mustard that was now ground into his shirt.

I felt my face burning. "Oh, jeez, I can't believe this!"

"*You* can't?"

He had every right to be mad, but when I looked up into his brown eyes, I could see that he was about to laugh. I could also see that he was . . . well, really cute. My heart started beating double-time, and my head felt light. "Let me get you some more napkins." For some reason, my throat had gone dry.

"Um — no, thanks," the cute boy said, a smile twitching at the edge of his mouth.

"I just want you to know that I'm usually very coordinated," I told him, instantly feeling like an idiot. *Stop talking*, I told myself. "I'm on the basketball team," I went on, instantly disobeying my own orders.

He grinned. "I would have guessed you were on the National Food Fight team."

Okay. Okay, he's joking. So at least he doesn't want to kill me. . . . "I used to be — but I got cut."

"Too many fouls?" Cute Boy guessed.

I nodded. "You got it."

Laughing, he looked down at his shirt. "This

isn't so bad, really. I can take care of it in the bathroom."

"Really?"

"Don't sweat it," he said, and I could have hugged him. Not that I'd ever do anything like that, of course.

I was still smiling when I got back to our table. Lindsay gave me a look as I sat down.

"Ooooh," she said playfully. "I saw that move! Pretty smooth, Nicolette Spicer."

I felt myself blushing again. "He was cool about it."

"Hmm. I don't know that I've ever seen you smiling so hard before."

"I wasn't smiling!" I insisted, a little too loudly. Some of the girls at the next table looked over. Andrea Flemming twirled a blond curl around her finger and whispered something to Yolanda Stewart, who giggled. Those two were always whispering about who-knows-what, but I dropped my voice, anyway. "I was just . . . talking."

"Oh, okay." Lindsay shrugged, playing with a curl that had escaped her doughnut 'do. "Then I guess you don't want to know who he is."

"Why? Do you know him?"

She cackled at the eagerness in my voice. "Look who isn't smiling!" Lindsay crowed.

I sighed, leaning back in my chair. Okay, here is the deal — Lindsay is the one with all the crushes. She changes interest in guys like she changes hairstyles — often. And she's always after me because I'm never crushing on anyone. So now, here I was, just having a conversation with someone who happened to be very cute . . . and she was positively *gleeful*.

"Okay, okay, since you're *begging* me, I'll tell you what I know," Lindsay said. "First, his name is Ben Reynolds."

"How do you know him?" Lindsay always seems to know everyone.

"He's on the tech crew for the play," she explained. "I've talked to him a couple of times. He's new — just started school in the fall. And he's got a great sense of humor."

"Anything else?"

"And he doesn't have a girlfriend."

My jaw dropped. "He *told* you that?"

"Not exactly," she admitted. "It's just a vibe. But don't worry, I'll get the whole scoop — since you're so interested!" She waggled her eyebrows.

"No — don't," I begged.

"Don't worry! I'll be subtle," Lindsay promised. It was no use, anyway. Once Lindsay made up her mind to do something, there was no talking her out of it.

I decided to change the subject. "Hey — I haven't heard *you* talk about anyone lately."

One shoulder went up, then dropped. "Eh."

"Isn't there anyone on your guy-dar?"

Lindsay looked down at the gray-green broccoli on her plate and gave it a tentative poke with her fork. "Not really. . . ." she hedged. "Well, maybe one guy, but . . . he doesn't like me in that way, so . . ."

"What do you mean?" I asked. "Who is it?"

Lindsay sighed. "I don't really want to talk about it."

I decided to leave it at that. Lindsay can never keep a secret long. I knew she'd tell me who she had her eye on, eventually.

I just hoped that she could keep *my* guy secret. For a little while, at least.

"I'm open!" I called as I danced at the edge of the paint, waving my hands like I was trying to flag down an airplane. "I'm open!"

Hannah Weaver ignored me, shoving her shoulder into Anita's in an attempt to shake her off. Anita is tall and thickly built, and when she leans on you, she doesn't move. Think "tree."

I saw Ivy's strawberry-blond bob flash by as she moved from defending Carla to trying to block Hannah's shot.

"Where are you going?" Carla called. "Come back!"

"I'm open!" I shouted again.

Has she been struck deaf? I wondered as Hannah's perfect features sorted themselves into a frown and she tried a little spin move. Then — unbelievably — she jumped and let the ball fly toward the basket.

"Go in, go in, go in!" Carla shouted as the ball tipped delicately around the edge of the rim. "Go —"

It went in. Of course.

"Yeah!" Carla dashed over to high-five Hannah.

Coach Chin blew her whistle as Hannah smiled, showing the dimple in her right cheek, and tugged at her perfect blond French braid. I ground my teeth, trying not to look annoyed.

"Okay, people, gather," Coach called, tucking a pencil behind her ear. She stood at the edge of the bleachers as we all gathered around her, panting like a pack of dogs. Coach Chin has been coaching the James Garfield Middle School girls' basketball team for nine years, and she has never, ever yelled at anyone in that time. She's the most controlled person I've ever met, from the razor part in her glossy black hair to the tips of her ultra-white tennis shoes. I'm not kidding, she's got shoes so white they're blinding. There's a rumor that Coach keeps them that bright to distract visiting teams.

"Hannah," Coach Chin said, "you need to pass to your teammates. Nick was open."

Thank you, I thought.

Hannah blinked, and her long brown lashes moved slowly. They made me think of butterfly wings pulsing at the edge of a blue flower. "The ball went in," Hannah said.

"You can't count on that in a game." Coach has eyes that are black, dark as the night sky. "You have to look for the open player. Take the game to where you're strongest."

"Okay." Hannah nodded, but the tips of her lips curled into a smirk, and I felt like I could almost read her thoughts.

Hannah's Brain: *What-ever. I'm the best shooter on the team, so deal.*

Grr.

I mean, I'm a good shooter, too. Hannah and I have almost identical percentages from the foul line. But she scores more points in games. Why? Because she's a ball hog!

She's like that off the court, too — all the guys

are crazy about her, and all the girls want to be her best friend. Or at least dress like her. Hannah is one of those athletic girls who manages to be a girly girl at the same time. Like, she never seems to break a sweat. Her hair is always bouncy and shiny, like in a shampoo commercial — even when she's running up and down the court. And when she's off the court, she dresses like she's got a personal shopper. It's annoying.

It's not that I'm jealous —

Well, not *exactly* that I'm jealous —

Okay, maybe a *little* jealous, but that's not the point.

I just want her to share the ball more, so that I can score once in a while. Is that too much to ask?

"I can't wait!"

"All the cuties are going to be there!"

"I heard that Stefan said he was going. Did you hear that Stefan was going?"

"Okay, but my closet is a disaster. Chi, what are you wearing?"

Around me, the locker room was fizzing like a Coca-Cola, with girls chattering away about some party. My head was still on the basketball court, though, so I just plastered a faint smile on my face and yanked off my on-court sneakers, pulled off my shorts, and slipped into my jeans. There was no point in switching my basketball jersey for a T-shirt, so I left it on. I'd shower at home.

I was tying the laces of my on-street sneakers when I heard Carla say, "Would somebody poke her, please?" and the next thing I knew, Anita had jabbed me in the shoulder.

"Ow," I said. "What?"

"I have been *trying* to get your attention for the past five minutes, Nick," Carla said dramatically. She really should have auditioned for the play instead of trying out for the basketball team.

"Okay. You've got it."

Carla tossed her curly black hair and said, "So — what are you wearing?"

What the heck kind of question is that? I wondered. "I'm wearing a pair of jeans and my basketball jersey — *duh.*"

"Not right *now,* jock-brain," Carla said as Ivy tossed a towel at my head. "To Hannah's party next Saturday!"

I ducked, and the towel flopped to the floor. "Oh." *Party? What party?* I looked at the eager faces of my teammates — it looked as if Hannah had invited almost everyone on the team. *Almost. . . .* "I don't think I'm invited."

"Of course you're invited!" Carla cried. "Everyone's invited! Isn't that right, Hannah?"

Hannah — who had at that very moment walked up to her locker — gave Carla an I-want-to-kill-you smile and said, "Sure." She was dressed, but her hair was wrapped in a towel, and she smelled sweet, like flowers.

"There you go." Totally oblivious to the fact that she had just strong-armed my invitation to Hannah's party from the hostess herself, Carla went on, "So what are you wearing? Not that basketball jersey, okay? Do you know what I'm saying?"

"Does Nick own anything but basketball jerseys?" Hannah asked. There was a sneer in her voice.

Too bad your personality isn't as pretty as your face, I thought.

"She owns soccer jerseys, too," Anita said, and I flashed her a look. Anita was one of my best friends on the team, and she grinned at me. "Sorry, Nick, but am I lying?"

Anita and Carla bumped fists, and I sighed. "I have no idea what to wear," I said, turning back to slam my locker. *Because I am not going to Hannah's stupid party*, I thought.

Hannah looked at me and a corner of her mouth

twitched up into a smile, like she knew what I was thinking, and she was glad.

"Let her wear the jersey," Ivy suggested. "I'm wearing my new skirt."

Carla slung her green athletic bag over her shoulder. "Oooh, can't wait to feast my eyes on that cutie, Ben Reynolds!"

It's just luck, pure and simple, that I didn't give myself whiplash at that moment, because I turned around so fast that I must have looked like a pinwheel on a stick. Ben Reynolds? Cute Boy? Punch-on-his-shirt-has-a-sense-of-humor-and-big-brown-eyes-and-no-girlfriend-or-so-Lindsay-thinks Ben? *Wait, wait, hold up.* I was beginning to rethink this party concept.

"He'll be there, right, Hannah?" Carla pressed. "And what about Stefan? Chi wanted to know about Stefan."

"Shut *up*!" Chi cried, giving Carla a playful punch on the arm. "Jeez, Carla, could you keep it zipped, for once?"

She was kidding, of course. Everyone knows the answer to that one: No.

"Of course they're coming, what do you think?" Hannah replied, like *Who on earth wouldn't want to come to my party?*

Well, good question, now that Ben was going to be there. And the next thing I knew, before my brain even had time to form actual words, I heard someone say, "So, Hannah, what day is the party again? What time? And what's your address?"

Hannah lifted her eyebrows, and I realized that the person with all the questions was me. "It's a week from Saturday," she said slowly. "The party starts at seven."

"Don't worry, Nick, I'll e-mail you the directions to Hannah's house," Carla said quickly. She grinned at Hannah.

A week from Saturday. Ten days from now. I had ten days to find something to wear to Hannah's party . . . because Ben was going to be there. *I'm going to a party with Ben!* I thought dizzily. *All I have to do is not spill anything on him!* "Great!" I told Hannah. I could feel the smile on my face — it was wider than my teeth. "It should be fun!"

"Sure it will," Hannah said. She didn't actually sound like she believed it, but I didn't care. I was going to get another chance to talk to Ben. That was all that mattered.

Opening lines scrolled through my mind like the headlines at the bottom of the TV screen — *Hey, how's your shirt? Isn't this a great party? Had any good food accidents lately?* — when I pushed open the door to the girls' locker room and came face-to-face with . . .

Ben.

"I know you," he said with a smile.

"Muh," I said as my lips stumbled over themselves in an attempt to say something. Then I laughed nervously. Over his shoulder, I caught sight of Lindsay standing several feet away. She was grinning and pointing at Ben, as if I might not have noticed he was there. I tried my best to ignore her.

"Looks like I caught you by surprise," Ben said. He jammed his hands into his pockets.

"I just . . . I just thought that you might have come by to squirt some mustard on me," I managed to joke. "You didn't, did you? This isn't some kind of revenge ambush, is it?"

Waggling her eyebrows, Lindsay gave me a thumbs-up. I resisted the urge to strangle her.

Ben smiled, and I noticed that he had a tiny crescent-shaped scar on his upper lip. It seemed to be pointing to his white, even teeth. "I'm unarmed," he said, holding up his hands. "I'm just here because I heard it's where all the cool people hang out."

"Oh, yeah, smelly gyms are totally in," I told him, and smiled to myself when he laughed. "I think there are a few A-list celebrities behind the bleachers."

"I thought you were the main A-lister around here," Ben replied. "I hear you're the star of the team."

"Who'd you hear that from?" I asked, even though I knew the answer. Little Miss *Subtle,* who was standing behind Ben, pointing to herself and grinning madly.

"I thought it was common knowledge," Ben told me.

"I like to think of myself as one of the Detroit Pistons," I told him. "They play real team ball."

"Those guys are fun to watch," Ben agreed. "But I have to admit that I'm a Jazz fan."

"Jazz?" I screeched in mock horror. "What about the home team?"

Laughing, Ben held up his hands, palms out, like he was surrendering. "The Nuggets are great. But I was born in Utah. Besides, I think it's the Jazz's year."

Behind him, Lindsay was showing how happy she was with this conversation by doing a little victory dance, as though I'd scored a touchdown or something.

"Ben, do you know my friend, Lindsay?" I asked, and Ben turned just in time to catch Lindsay mid-dance, one hand up in the air, one hip out to the side. Lindsay froze.

Hee-hee! I thought. *Got you back!*

"Hi, Ben!" Lindsay said brightly. Then she put her other hand in the air and bent over her legs. "Mmm, this stretch feels great! I've been sitting backstage for an hour, and boy, am I stiff. You guys should try it."

"Lindsay and I are working on the play together," Ben explained.

"No kidding," I said dryly.

At that very moment, I heard the door behind me open, and a familiar voice say, "Oh, great, you're here."

"Hey, Hannah," Ben said smoothly as she stepped up beside him.

Hold the phone . . . had Ben been waiting here — for her?

"Hi, Hannah!" Lindsay chirped.

Hannah barely glanced in her direction, just gave her a mini-nod. "You ready?" she asked Ben. "I need to get out of here. I'm starving."

Hesitating, Ben glanced at me, then shrugged. "Sure," he said. "I'm ready. I'll see you guys later, okay?"

"See you," Lindsay called after their retreating forms as they headed for the gym's exit.

I didn't say anything. I couldn't.

"She's not his girlfriend," Lindsay said. Reading my mind, as usual.

I looked at her. "You asked him that?" I demanded.

"Okay, so she's not *necessarily* his girlfriend," Lindsay admitted. "They're probably just in a car pool or something."

But I had a bad feeling. "Hannah's having a party," I said. "She said that Ben would be there."

"Hmm." Lindsay glanced through the large glass windows that lined the edge of the gym as Ben and Hannah walked down the hall, toward the school's side exit. "Guys do tend to go for the tall, blond, evil ones," she admitted.

I lifted an eyebrow.

"What?" she demanded. "I read that in a magazine! Okay, look, just because he hangs out with Hannah doesn't mean that they're together. They could be cousins. Or just friends. Or — like — in a club together. Or a car pool, like I said before. Or he could be her math tutor —"

"All right, all right," I said at last. "I get it."

"I'm telling you, he really seemed to like talking to you," Lindsay said. She looked really earnest.

I studied her face, her wide hazel eyes with flecks of yellow. It's a funny thing — we look completely different. I have dark hair and dark eyes, and Lindsay is a redhead. But people always mistake us for sisters. I actually have a twin — but he's a brother, not a sister. In a way, I like to think of Lindsay as my almost-sister. That's how well she knows me . . . and how well I know her. "You're just telling me that so I won't be upset," I said.

"I know," Lindsay agreed.

"You're a good friend, Lindsay Sweet," I told her.

"I know that, too." Lindsay grinned. "Now let's go get some ice cream."

DAY TWO

FRiDAY

QUIZ: What Does He Really Think of You?

When he sees you in the hall, he:

A. blushes madly and runs in the opposite direction.

B. gives you a thousand-megawatt smile.

C. asks to copy your homework — again.

D. waves at you with one arm as he wraps the other around the head cheerleader's shoulders.

E. pretends he doesn't even see you!

"Over here!" I called, dumping my gym bag at the edge of the driveway.

Alex tossed me the basketball without even looking, and I ran in for the layup — which he rejected. He sent it sailing across the lawn.

"In your face! Your game's so weak, it can't lift a finger to dial the doctor." Alex grinned. He's my twin, but he's still taller than I am — and better on defense. Which is why I learned to play such tough offense. "Oh, hey, Lindsay," he said, his ears turning red. Embarrassed by his own goofy trash-talk. Serves him right.

Lindsay laughed. "Hi." I chased after the ball, and Lindsay flopped onto the grass, her wide black Indian skirt ballooning around her.

"You staying over?" Alex asked her.

"Just picking up Nick's bag — she's spending the night at my place." Lindsay gathered her long red hair at the base of her neck and tied it into a knot. I think that is so cool, but it's completely impossible with my hair. Not just because it's short — because it's too slidey. The knot would slip right out.

"That's cool. Steve and I are going to see the new movie at the multi." Alex grabbed the ball out of the air as I tossed it to him. "If you guys want to come along."

Lindsay looked at me, like she was kind of interested, but I said, "We rented some stuff," which was true. Lindsay and I had picked up two movies — a comedy and an action flick I'd been dying to see. I didn't mind hanging out with my brother. He's cool. But his friend Steve can be a major know-it-all, which seriously works my nerves sometimes.

"Maybe next time," Lindsay said.

Alex jumped, hooking a nifty little shot into the hoop that our parents had attached to the garage two years ago. I grabbed the rebound and lined up right where he'd been standing. Same shot: *Swish.*

"Just give me a second to school this guy," I said to Lindsay.

"Oh, please," Alex teased as he grabbed the ball. "My game's so slick, it makes people fall over." He dribbled the ball through his legs, showing off.

"Your game's so feeble, old ladies help it across the street," I shot back. This is our little game. Trash-talk is much more fun than HORSE.

"You won't be saying that when you see my next move," Alex promised.

"This should be good for a laugh," I told him with a snort. "Do you mind hanging out a little while?" I asked Lindsay.

She leaned back on her elbows. "Take your time. I've got some questions for Alex, anyway."

"Questions for me?" Alex stumbled a little as he headed toward the basket for his next shot, which is probably why it clanged off the rim.

"My lead," I said, grabbing the ball. I ran toward the hoop and moved into a tight twist — a fancy new layup I'd been practicing.

"So, Alex," Lindsay said. "What do guys like in a girl?"

Clang!

"Lindsay!" I screeched.

"What?" Lindsay blinked at me innocently. "Alex is a guy — this is research!"

I glanced at my twin, who looked like he was about to die of embarrassment. He wasn't the only one.

Lindsay and I had been talking about this very subject as we walked home that afternoon. More specifically, we'd discussed whether guys ever went for jock-ish girls. Maybe that was why Hannah always went out of her way to seem extra girly.

"What do —?" Alex had caught the ball, but when he tried to dribble it, it bounced away from him. Darting after it, he managed to recover a little and then stood still, giving Lindsay a careful look. My brother always wears baggy clothes, and today was no exception. He had on loose shorts and a navy blue T-shirt that was about two sizes too big. Tucking the ball under his arm, he asked, "Um — why? Why do you — uh — want to know?"

I rolled my eyes. This was ridiculous. "Alex isn't a guy, Lindsay. He's my brother," I pointed out.

"He's still a *guy*," Lindsay insisted. "I'm just looking for the male point of view."

"Alex is standing right here," Alex said, waving with his right hand.

I threw my hands in the air. "Okay, Alex, what do guys like in a girl?"

Alex ran a hand through his hair, pulling his floppy bangs out of his face. Alex has long hair. It's almost to his shoulders. "I don't know," he said.

I turned to Lindsay. "See?"

"Well, think about it," Lindsay prompted.

"I guess . . . uh . . . I like it when . . ." Alex shrugged. "Uh . . . when girls smell nice. . . ."

"When they smell nice?" I repeated. What kind of advice was that?

Lindsay gave me a knowing look, and I realized that I was still sweaty and disgusting from basketball practice . . . and I had been when I saw Ben yesterday afternoon, too. *I always wait until I get home to shower*, I thought, *but maybe that's not such a great idea*. My shirt was still totally soaked under the armpits, and my hair was sticking to my face. I blew a lock out of my mouth. Hmm. Maybe this advice wasn't so bad after all.

"So you like perfume?" Lindsay pressed.

"Uh, I guess." He tucked his lips together.

"What about makeup?" Lindsay asked.

"Oh, I hate makeup," Alex said. "I like it when girls look natural."

I nodded. *Oh-kay*, I thought. *I'm already down with the natural look. All I ever use is lip balm.*

Lindsay rolled her eyes and pulled a magazine out of her bag. "Natural — like this?" she asked, holding up the cover.

Shifting his weight from one foot to the other, Alex glanced at the picture. "Sure, she's pretty, I guess. See — she doesn't have on any makeup."

"Alex," I snapped, "she's wearing purple eye shadow!"

"She *is*?" Alex squinted harder at the picture.

Lindsay lifted her eyebrows at me and nodded. "Okay," she said. "Thanks." This was exactly what Lindsay had been telling me earlier — she'd just read that most guys *think* they like the natural look, but what they really like is natural-looking makeup.

Alex tossed the ball in my direction, but I passed it back. "I think we're about to head."

"Really?" Alex looked disappointed as Lindsay scrambled to her feet.

"Yeah," I said. "Lindsay's mom is expecting us for dinner."

"Okay." He shrugged again, making his baggy T-shirt flutter slightly. "See you guys."

"See you," Lindsay said as Alex tossed the ball toward the hoop. *Swish*. "You know, we really don't have to rush," she added in a low voice as we headed toward the side door.

"I know," I told her. I yanked open the door and stood aside to let her into the kitchen. "I just suddenly felt like I wanted to jump in the shower."

I flopped against the giant multicolored pillow in the corner of Lindsay's bedroom while she paged through a pile of magazines spread across the floor in front of her. Glossy smiles gleamed up at me as headlines screamed: "Lose Five Pounds Fast!" and "Get His Attention, Now!" and "Your Homework Headaches — Solved!" Lindsay's magazines promised to fix all my problems — a few of which I hadn't even realized I had. No wonder people bought them. A couple of these magazines, and your life could be absolutely perfect.

"How cool would it be to put the Wicked Witch in something like this?" Lindsay asked, holding up a magazine and tapping the back with her finger.

A glittery, poufy, orange floor-length dress twinkled at me from the page. "The Wicked Witch meets prom in 1980," I said. "It's different."

"It would totally pop against her green skin." Lindsay peered down at the picture again. "I could put Glinda in a black cocktail dress and the Wicked

Witch in this crazy thing, and totally blow people's minds!" She grinned at me.

Oh, boy, I thought. Mr. Logan, the drama teacher, had told Lindsay that she could do whatever she wanted. He'd told her to "think beyond the aquarium in which we swim," whatever that meant. *Man, is he going to be sorry.*

"I don't know if she'll be very scary in that," I pointed out.

"Mmmm." Lindsay mashed her lips together, thinking. "Good point," she said at last, tossing the magazine aside. It flopped closed, and a headline on the cover caught my eye. QUIZ: IN A GUY'S EYES! HOW DOES HE SEE YOU? PAGE 52! Without even thinking, I picked it up and turned to page 52.

"Do you think the Munchkins should have a disco theme?" Lindsay asked as she flipped pages at warp speed.

"Hippies would make more sense," I said absently as I read the first question.

When you talk to a guy, you're most likely to:

A. ask for his digits in the first five seconds.

B. ask if he wants to shoot some hoops.

C. ask a lot of questions to see what he's interested in.

D. Talk to a guy? Forget it!

Well, obviously B. I marked down the answer in the margin.

"Hippies?" Lindsay asked.

"You know — flower children?" I told her. "Isn't that what Munchkins are, kind of? Don't they live in flowers?"

"Nick, you're a total genius!" Lindsay scribbled something on a yellow pad and moved on to the next magazine. She was babbling something about the Cowardly Lion, how it was female lions that actually did all the hunting in nature, so it wasn't really that weird that the male lion was a sissy, while I skimmed the rest of the quiz. B, B, B, B, B. All my answers were Bs. After seven questions, I skipped to the end of the quiz, to the scoring section. I read aloud, "If you answered mostly B, you tend to see guys as buddies, and that's probably how they see you, too. You're one of the guys!"

One of the guys? I thought. *That's not what I want to be!* I flipped the page to see if there were any tips on how to change that, but the next article was about the hottest new winter coats. Like that was any help.

"Are you actually reading that magazine?" Lindsay asked. Rolling over, she propped her head on her hand.

I shrugged. "Sure."

Lindsay laughed. "Seriously? I've known you since forever, and you have never — not once — picked up one of my magazines."

"Well, maybe that's my problem," I said dryly.

"What?" Lindsay shook her head. "What do you mean?"

I sighed. "Didn't you hear me? This stupid quiz says that guys tend to see me as a buddy."

Lindsay rolled her eyes. "And that's some kind of news flash?"

"Thanks a lot!" I tossed the magazine, and she ducked, giggling. It whacked the foot of her bed instead. Yanking the pillow from behind me, I hugged it to my chest. "It's just that — when I saw Ben walk off with Hannah the other day . . ."

"Yeah." Lindsay sighed. "But I still say she isn't his girlfriend," she added.

"Maybe not, but she's the kind guys go for, right? This kind of girl?" I pointed to the cover of *Teen Scene*. "The girls on the team were right — I can't just wear a soccer jersey to Hannah's party and expect to get Ben to talk to me instead of her." I'd told Lindsay all about the party, of course.

"Well, that's easy to fix," Lindsay said. "We'll just make you so gorgeous that he has to talk to you instead of her!"

"Right."

"I mean it!"

"And how are we going to do that?" I asked, but Lindsay was already pawing through magazines.

"Aren't I head makeup artist at school?" she demanded. "I'll give you a makeover! Okay, we want something glamorous . . . here!" Crawling across the floor, she hauled a huge tackle box out of her closet and flipped it open. Inside were pans of foundation, eyeliner, brilliant eye shadow colors, blush, a fake nose, a couple of warts, some tooth black, a mustache — the works. "Okay, we have to start with a base," she said, pulling out a sponge and some thick pancake makeup. She frowned at me, then swabbed the sponge in the makeup and started attacking my face, smearing goop all over it.

"That feels gross," I told her.

"It'll even out your skin tone and provide a base on which to apply the rest of the makeup," she said, as if she'd read that in a book somewhere.

"It feels like my face is covered in slime."

"You'll get used to it," she promised, reaching for a small round box of something green.

I ducked away from the makeup. "Whoa — you aren't turning me into the Wicked Witch, are you?"

"It's eye shadow," Lindsay said. "It makes brown eyes pop." She dusted some lightly on my lids with a brush. "Open," she commanded briskly, and I did.

"Oh, they'll definitely see you from the back of the theater now."

"Is that what I want?"

Lindsay ignored me. "Look at the ceiling." Then she tried to stick something black in my eye.

"Get that away from me!" I cried, batting at her hand.

"It's eyeliner! You have to have eyeliner! I'm not putting it in your eye, I promise."

I blinked a lot, but she finally managed to get some on me. Then she whisked on some mascara and leaned back to survey her work.

"It's not quite right," Lindsay said, cocking her head to the side. She looked down at the magazine, as though it had given her bad advice. "Hmm. . . . You have nice eyes, Nick. Maybe they'd look bigger with false eyelashes." She nodded. "Definitely."

She dabbed some eyelash glue on the rims of two spidery-looking things, then stuck them at the edges of my eyelids. Then she told me to suck in my cheeks as she brushed some candy-apple coloring on my cheekbone. "To give you a rosy glow," she said.

"Isn't it too bright?"

"If it isn't bright enough, it won't show up," Lindsay said. "Okay, now a little lipstick. What do you think of a beauty mark?"

"Holy guacamole, Lindsay, what on earth are you doing to Nick's face?"

Looking up, I saw Lindsay's sisters, Tracy and Stacy, standing in the doorway. They were both in high school, one year apart. Tracy had long blond hair that hung like a glossy curtain down her back. She was wearing narrow jeans that fit like tights and a clingy T-shirt. Stacy had on leopard-print leggings under a black skirt and a couple of shirts in neutral colors layered over each other. Her curly light-brown hair was piled on top of her head and held with a chopstick. They looked like they had stepped out of Lindsay's magazines.

"Are you auditioning to be a Vegas showgirl?" Stacy asked sarcastically.

"Yeah, or like, sending Nick to clown college?" Tracy added.

"Good one," Stacy said, and the two high-fived.

Lindsay's face was burning. "I'm giving Nick a makeover."

"Are you serious?" Tracy demanded.

"Great new look, Lindsay," Stacy put in. "It's a Halloween celebration every day."

"What did you use to apply that foundation?" Tracy snorted. "A spatula?"

"Good one," Stacy said, and the two high-fived again.

"This is stupid," I said, standing up. "I don't know what I was thinking."

"Well, if you were thinking that you need to lose the twelve-year-old-style-impaired-boy-look, you're on to something," Stacy said as she stepped into the room. "Your problem isn't your face — your problem is your clothes. But you shouldn't have let Lindsay help you."

"One look at her should have told you that she doesn't know anything about fashion," Tracy agreed.

"Hey!" Lindsay cried.

"I'm getting the makeup remover," Tracy said as she hurried down the hall.

"Bring the whole bag of cotton balls!" Stacy called after her. Folding her arms, she stood back and studied me.

I shifted from one leg to another. "Um . . ."

"Okay, number one, when you wear a sack, you look like a sack," Stacy announced out of the blue. "You've got to wear something with a little shape, Nick."

"She's got nice legs," Tracy said, walking in with the makeup remover and a makeup bag. "You should try skirts." She squirted some white goo on a cotton ball and started dabbing at my face.

"And choose clothes that give you a waist." Stacy nodded.

"She's got nice skin," Tracy said, peering at my face. She tossed a disgusting brown-and-black cotton ball onto the yellow carpet and dampened another one. "Tiny pores."

This was truly weird. I felt like a side of beef or a prize pig. Something to be inspected, poked at, measured up.

"Oh, you are *so* lucky," Stacy told me, sitting down daintily on Lindsay's blue-and-white cloud bedspread. "My pores are huge."

I felt an odd flash of pride at my pore size. I'd never even *noticed* my pores before.

"You don't need foundation," Tracy proclaimed. "Probably not even eyeliner — not for every day, at least. Just a little mascara," she said, sweeping some onto my upper lashes. "Lindsay, what were you thinking with the green eye shadow?"

"I thought it was in," Lindsay said meekly.

"Oh, please — tons of ugly things are in. You don't see me wearing ankle boots, do you?" Stacy demanded. "I'm going to get Nick something to wear."

"Get something for Lindsay, too," Tracy suggested.

"Something for me?" Lindsay looked shocked. "I don't need a makeover!"

Stacy lifted an eyebrow at her. "You're kidding, right?"

"Only celebrities can pull off the bag-lady look," Tracy said as she spread some pink lip gloss onto my lips.

"Bag lady?" Lindsay cried.

"Oh, please." Tracy brushed some pale pink blush onto my cheeks. "That outfit looks like you picked it out of a Dumpster."

"Good one!" Stacy called from down the hall.

"Nick!" Lindsay was looking to me for support, but I had to admit that her sisters had a point. Lindsay's long black Indian skirt was wrinkled, and she had on a scroungy T-shirt that said ROCK STAR that I happened to know came from the Goodwill. She was wearing heavy black boots that laced up the front.

I winced. "Sorry."

Stacy came back with a pile of clothes. A simple pink dress for Lindsay, black leggings, a denim skirt, and a fitted T-shirt for me. "You could wear a little makeup, too — but not that hideous red lipstick," Stacy told her sister, and went to work on Lindsay's face while Tracy smeared something on her hands, then started working it through my hair.

"I don't like junk in my hair," I told her.

She just gave me a doubtful look, then went on with what she was doing.

"Ouch!" Lindsay cried.

"Hold still!" Stacy commanded, holding up a pair of tweezers. "Your eyebrows need shape!"

Twenty minutes later, I stood beside Lindsay in front of her full-length mirror.

"What do you think?" Tracy asked.

I thought that Lindsay looked amazing. Stacy had straightened her long red hair, and it looked glossy and perfect, just like Tracy's. I don't know what Stacy did to Lindsay's eyes, but I'd never noticed how hazel they were before. The pink dress made her skin look warm. She looked really pretty.

"You look so gorgeous," Lindsay told me.

"I do?" It wasn't that I didn't believe her — it was that I barely even recognized the person in the mirror as *me*. This person had clothes that really fit, and Tracy and Stacy had been right — the skirt showed off my legs. I guess all that basketball had paid off somehow. My hair was fluffed up in back, and Tracy had put a line of sparkly little barrettes at my part, just over my bangs. The mascara made my brown eyes look huge. I looked cool. I looked like . . . I looked like a girl.

A girly girl.

"You're *wel*-come," Stacy singsonged.

"You guys can borrow those clothes tomorrow, if you want," Tracy offered.

"But if you spill anything on them, you are so totally dead," Stacy added.

"What do you think?" Lindsay turned to me. She was smiling hugely as she grabbed my hands.

What did I think? I thought that if I went to Hannah's party looking like this, Ben would definitely notice me. It wasn't really my look . . . but it was a good look.

I also thought that I didn't have a single item in my wardrobe that looked like these clothes. I didn't have any makeup, either. But that was okay. I had nine days to get that stuff. Nine days until Hannah's party.

"I think we need to do some shopping," I said.

DAY THREE

SATURDAY

QUIZ: Hippie Chick, Perfect Prep, or Divine Diva? Find Your True Style!

When it comes to accessories, your motto is:

A. "No leather, no fur. Only cruelty-free products for me."

B. "Simple and classic makes the look."

C. "Too much is never enough!"

D. "Accessories? You mean I have to do something besides getting dressed?"

"Am I doing this right?" I asked as I smeared lip gloss over my lips the next morning. I felt like a kindergartener having trouble staying inside the lines. I frowned at myself in Lindsay's mirror. "This looks a lot gloppier than when Tracy did it."

"Makeup is all about practice," Lindsay said as she brushed her hair. "When we did Frankenstein last year, it took me forever to get all the scars and stuff to look right."

I thought that giving myself fake scars might be better somehow — I'd probably feel less annoyed if they didn't turn out perfect. I fiddled with the glittery barrettes in my hair. Really, I hadn't re-done the makeup, hair, and outfit as well as Tracy had the first time, but I still looked okay. Pretty, even.

It was strange to see that face in the mirror that was mine, but not mine, too. *Who are you?* I thought at myself.

I'm Nicolette, the girl in the mirror thought back, which caught me off guard. Nicolette. That was my name — my real name. Was the girl in the mirror the real me, then? I'd have to get to know her a little better to find out.

"Wake up, wake up, wake up!" The door banged open and Alex barged into Lindsay's room, grinning. He stopped when he saw me.

Lindsay grabbed an orange throw pillow from her bed and tossed it at his head. "Alex, what if we were getting dressed in here?" she cried.

He deflected the pillow with no problem, and it fell to the floor. He blinked at Lindsay, standing there in her pink dress. "Mom and I are here to pick up Nick," he said absently, shaking his head. "What are you wearing?"

Lindsay rolled her eyes. "It's called a dress."

My twin turned to me. "What happened to you guys?"

I snorted. "We got makeovers, you knucklehead!"

Alex looked from me to Lindsay. "Why?"

Thanks a lot, I thought. *Brothers*. Ignoring the question, I stood up and walked over to zip up my bag just as Mom walked through the door. If you hadn't noticed, my family and Lindsay's are pretty tight. Mi casa es su casa, and all that.

"Good morning, sweeties!" Mom chirped. "Oh, my goodness, don't you two look darling! Lindsay, that is just the cutest little dress!" Mom was wearing her usual jeans and soft sweater, plus boots with a heel. She's very into heels, my mother. She's only five feet tall, so she doesn't step out of the house without her "proper shoes." Thank goodness I take after my dad, who is six foot two. It's better for basketball.

"Thanks, Mrs. Spicer," Lindsay said, smiling shyly.

"And Nick, you look simply adorable! Turn around, so I can see you!" Mom smiled, showing her dimples. She has the prettiest smile.

I spun obediently while my mother clucked at how "fashionable" and "in" my clothes were. "And just so flattering, Nick!" she gushed.

"Can we go?" Alex asked. "I'm supposed to be at Rick's house in ten minutes." My brother, Mr. Popularity. His weekends are always booked with a thousand plans.

"Hold on a minute, I've got to show Dad," Mom said, digging around in her bag for her camera phone. "You two stand together." She waved for me to move in next to Lindsay. "Did Andrea see you?" Mom asked as she took the picture. She meant Lindsay's mom.

"She saw us last night," I said.

"After Tracy and Stacy got hold of us," Lindsay added.

"That explains it," Alex said, rolling his eyes. He's not wild about Lindsay's older sisters — he thinks they're stuck-up. Which they kind of are, but still.

"Well, you girls look just fantastic," Mom said. "Just adorable! Like you stepped right out of *Teen Scene* magazine! Nick, I just can't get over seeing you in a skirt — you have great legs! Doesn't she, Alex?"

"This is getting weird," Alex muttered.

Have I mentioned that my mother is really into fashion? She's consistently the best-dressed teacher at the school where she works. And she's been trying to get me to ditch the "tomboy" look for ages. Seeing me in a skirt was probably a dream come true for her.

Lindsay nudged me with her elbow, and I said, "Mom — would you take me and Lindsay to the mall today?"

"'Lindsay and me,'" Mom corrected automatically — it's the English teacher in her, she can't help it — "and I would be *delighted* to take you girls shopping, just tickled pink!"

"Don't forget to drop me off first," Alex said.

I grabbed my bag. "Don't worry — we won't be looking for *your* opinion."

"This is going to be so much fun!" Lindsay said with a huge smile.

"Won't it?" Mom agreed. "Oh, it'll be perfectly dee-lightful! Won't it, Nick?"

I laughed, but I had to agree. I think this was the first time in my life that I'd actually looked forward to a shopping trip.

Mom's heels clicked on the marble floor as we made our way through the maze of makeup and fragrance counters on the first floor of her favorite department store, Bennett & Browning. Flowery smells wafted past my nose. I made the mistake of making eye contact with a woman standing next to the escalator, and she squirted me with something that smelled like mulch and roses. Ick.

"We'll go straight to see Marilyn," Mom said, as we floated over the buzzing makeup floor on the escalator. "She's been helping me pick out clothes for the past five years."

Lindsay nodded eagerly at me. *Marilyn:* The name conjured up classic movie stars and sophisticated glamour. *And my mom is always well dressed,* I reasoned. "Sounds great," I told her.

"Annette!" A woman with funky, cropped white hair and glasses on a beaded chain greeted my mother as we walked into the women's section. She had on a black turtleneck sweater and a long black skirt — sophisticated and elegant.

"Hi, Marilyn!" Mom chirped. "Oh, where did you get that bracelet?" she asked, gesturing to the gold cuff on Marilyn's wrist. "It's divine!"

"Thank you!" Marilyn peered at us through her glasses, which made her blue eyes seem enormous. "And who is this?"

"This is my daughter, Nicolette," Mom said, nudging me forward a little. My shoulder brushed a rack of silk shirts, nearly knocking one to the floor, but I managed to catch it and hang it back before it fell. "And her best friend and my 'second daughter,' Lindsay."

"Hi!" Lindsay said. "I love your beaded eyeglass chain."

"I made it myself," Marilyn told her.

"Cool!" Lindsay beamed.

"The girls need some new clothes," my mother explained. "The basics for a new wardrobe. They're growing up!" Her eyes got a little misty at that remark, and I patted her shoulder.

"Don't I know it!" Marilyn said. "All right." The saleslady folded one arm across her waist and propped up the other to tap at her lips. "I suggest we go with a neutral palette. Lots of muted separates that can all be worn together."

"Sounds fantastic!" Mom said. "That's the way I'd go. Okay, sweeties, I'm going to browse around. Let me know when you're ready to try things on — I want to see how you look!"

Mom wandered over to a rack of blouses at the back of the department while Marilyn sized us up.

"Nicolette, I think you should head more toward a navy base," Marilyn said as she grabbed a blazer off the rack behind Lindsay. "And for Lindsay, I think we'll work with a brown. Maybe mix it up for both of you with some jewel tones." With that, she grabbed a red silk shirt with a bow at the neck and held it up. "I just got one of these for my daughter. Red is everywhere these days."

Lindsay glanced at me dubiously. I could read her thoughts: *A blouse with a bow? Are we, like, going to work for Corporate America?*

"And these navy pants are *perfection*," Marilyn continued as she bustled around the department.

Marilyn grabbed about a thousand coordinating clothes and started hanging them in our dressing rooms as Lindsay and I walked around awkwardly.

"I kind of like this," Lindsay said, touching a tiger-striped blouse. "You know, if it weren't dry clean only. And button-down. And without the collar. Maybe in a different fabric."

I picked up the sleeve and looked at the tag. "It's more than a hundred dollars!"

Lindsay stepped away from the blouse as if it was on fire.

"Girls!" Marilyn singsonged. "Come try on a few things! I'll go get your mother."

Dutifully, we trudged into the dressing room. *Why do they always have to have such hideous lighting in department stores?* I wondered as I caught a glimpse of myself in the mirror. I looked positively green.

"This one's for Lindsay," Marilyn said, gesturing to a door with a brown tweed skirt hanging on the door. "And you're in here, Nicolette."

My dressing room was hung with four blouses

in different tones, a navy skirt, a navy long-sleeved dress, and the navy pants Marilyn had picked out. Solid-colored sweaters were stacked up on the bench that sat between panels of the three-way mirror. I sighed. These clothes weren't exactly exciting. On the other hand, maybe Marilyn was on the right track — we needed to start with basics.

I peeled off my — well, Tracy's — shirt and skirt and stepped into the navy pants, then put on the red shirt with the bow. Standing back, I surveyed myself in the mirror. I felt like Lawyer Barbie.

"How's it going?" Mom's voice asked.

"Um, okay," I said, gazing at my reflection. The clothes fit — technically. But . . .

"Come out so that we can take a look!" Mom said.

I peeked out of my dressing room and saw Lindsay emerge from hers in an orange sweater, brown skirt, and brown jacket. Two words popped into my mind: Librarian Lindsay.

Mom's smile flickered uncertainly. "That looks . . . very nice."

"It does?" Lindsay sounded dubious.

"Elegant." Marilyn nodded. "Sophisticated."

"Nick," Mom said, turning to me, "I just love that blouse — I may have to borrow it!" She glanced nervously in Marilyn's direction, as if she was worried about hurting her feelings.

"Um, Mom . . ." I hesitated. "Don't you think these clothes are a little . . ."

"They're building blocks for a versatile wardrobe," Marilyn said.

"Yeah," Lindsay agreed. "But don't we kind of look like we should be handing out cash behind the counter at the local bank?"

Mom looked at Marilyn, who blinked in surprise, then gave a little laugh.

"How old are you girls?" Marilyn asked. "I've gotten very bad at guessing ages."

"We're twelve," I told her.

"Actually, we're twelve next month," Lindsay volunteered.

"Oh, dear." A smile played on Marilyn's mouth as she cast a glance at my mother. The two burst into laughter.

"Marilyn, I think the girls need something more their age — more like what they were wearing when we got here."

Marilyn held up her hands. "I'm out of my league," she admitted, and I wanted to hug her.

"Mom, maybe Lindsay and I can look around on our own," I suggested.

Mom smiled. "Honey, I think that's a good idea. I think I'll look around here for a while. I can meet up with you later."

I breathed a huge sigh of relief. "Sounds perfect," I told her. *I really do have the world's coolest mom,* I thought.

"I'll give you some money," Mom said, digging around in her purse. "Lindsay, do you need some cash? I can call your mother and ask how much she wants me to give you."

"No, thanks, Mrs. Spicer," Lindsay said. "I brought my holiday money. Sorry, Marilyn."

"Oh, darling, you have to love what you're wearing or what's the point?" Marilyn said. "You girls can come back and see me when you've graduated from college."

"Now take off those clothes," Mom commanded, and Lindsay and I hurried to comply. "But leave the red blouse, Nick."

I paused at the door to the dressing room. I hesitated. "Mom, I really don't think it's me."

"Of course it isn't," Mom said. "I want to try it on!"

"It'll look darling on you," Marilyn told her.

Mom grinned. "Don't I know it!"

★ ★ ★

"I don't know." Lindsay and I were standing in front of Le Monde du Mode. "Isn't this place a little — expensive?" I asked.

"Ashley Violetta buys all her clothes at this store!" Lindsay insisted. "Well, at the Beverly Hills one, anyway."

"Ashley Violetta is a movie star with a seven-figure salary," I pointed out. "She's in all your magazines. She's released three CDs and is dating the lead singer of the Jams. We're not Ashley Violetta."

"Not *yet,*" Lindsay corrected. "Think of this as a reconnaissance mission."

"I don't know," I repeated, eyeing the window display. There was something about the luxe boutique that was making me hesitate. Maybe it was the mannequins dressed in shabby-looking rags that I knew must cost a thousand dollars, or maybe it was the brilliant lighting that called attention to the fact that the store was empty — nobody could afford to shop there, I guess — but I felt like there was a big NICOLETTE SPICER, YOU DO NOT BELONG IN HERE sign in the window.

"It's just a store," Lindsay said. "It's open to the public. Anyone can go in. Besides, it'll be fun." Grabbing my hand, she dragged me inside.

Our entrance set off a little *ding-dong,* and a moment later, we heard a *click-click-click* as a saleslady appeared, clacking her high heels against the slick floor. She looked like a supermodel — tall and slim and dressed all in black. Her brown hair flowed down her back, and her perfectly plucked brows were raised halfway up her forehead in anticipation of rich customers. When she saw us, the smile dropped right off of her face, and I could practically read her thoughts as though they were being broadcast across her forehead: *Oh, it's just a couple of kids.*

I glanced over at Lindsay, who had caught the same vibe I had, I could tell. But she chose to ignore it, traipsing over to a rack of dresses near the entrance.

"Hello," the saleslady said slowly, like she was trying to figure out just how rude she could be to us.

"Um, hello," I said quickly, before skulking over to a stack of colorful fitted T-shirts that looked just like what I was wearing at the moment. I picked one up and the tag fell out of the collar. Eighty dollars. For a T-shirt! *Whoa. I wonder if it's made of gold thread or something,* I thought. I put it back and headed toward the pants.

The saleslady walked over to the counter and

leaned lazily against the edge. “Is there anything I can help you girls find?” she asked, emphasizing the word “girls.” Translation: *Get out, stupid kids.*

Lindsay looked at me, and I was just about to suggest that we get going, when she narrowed her eyes in a look I knew well. Maybe a little too well. It was Lindsay’s I’m-up-to-something look. “Not yet, but we’ll let you know,” Lindsay said brightly.

In a British accent.

The saleslady sighed and glanced toward the door at the back of the store, like she wanted to get back to reading her magazine or something.

Lindsay pulled a green shimmery dress off of the rack and held it up. “Adrianna, what do you think of this?”

It took about fifteen seconds for me to realize that she was talking to *me.* “Er — it’s — pretty,” I said.

“Really?” Lindsay drew out the first syllable in a very English way and exhaled through her nose, her nostrils flaring slightly. “You think so? I’ve got this very dress at home, and I *never* wear it. It bunches at the shoulder in a way I can’t stand.” The hanger clicked as she set it back on the rack.

The saleslady looked dubious. “You have that dress?” she asked. “We just got it in the store last Thursday.”

Lindsay lifted an eyebrow. "Really? Then I suppose the Beverly Hills store gets its stock a little earlier than this one, because it's been hanging in my closet for three weeks. Do you like it, Adrianna? I'll give it to you, if you want it."

The saleslady's mouth dropped open a little, exposing her bottom row of perfectly white teeth, and she straightened up a little. She was starting to buy Lindsay's act.

Which wasn't that surprising, really. Even *I* was starting to buy it.

I had to bite the inside of my cheek to keep from giggling. This saleslady had brought out Lindsay's dramarama, and there was no putting it back now. "I look terrible in green, you know that," I told her, playing along.

Lindsay sighed. "Well, I suppose maybe the maid will want it."

"Are you looking for dresses?" the saleslady asked, perking up a little. "We have a few new ones over here." She led Lindsay to a rack near the back and held up a simple brown dress that looked like it was made of wool. It had unfinished edges at the hem and a cool brown-and-white pattern at the waist and cuffs.

"Yes, Jean-Paul showed me this one," Lindsay

said in her clipped fake accent. "It's darling, really, but I think it's just not me."

The saleslady looked intrigued. "Jean-Paul?"

"My stylist," Lindsay explained, tossing her red hair.

"Oh." The saleslady smiled in approval.

"Oh, Madeline!" I called. Lindsay smiled over at me as I held up one of the eighty-dollar T-shirts. "What do you think of these?"

Lindsay rolled her eyes. "I've got a closet stuffed with them," she said. "Frankly, they're comfortable, but I think they're done to death. I don't really expect that style to last beyond this season, do you?" she asked the saleslady.

"Oh, well, I —"

"Has silk simply gone out of fashion?" Lindsay went on, pulling out a pair of red pants with white roses on them. "You know, I see so many pants, and it seems as if they're all made of *polyester.*" She made *polyester* sound like *burlap.*

The saleslady looked flustered. "I think that —"

Lindsay cut her off. "You know, I really don't see anything here that just screams, 'Buy me!' Do you, Adrianna?"

I sighed. "I'm tempted by this," I said, holding up a peach suede jacket that cost more than a thousand dollars. "But if I put anything else on the credit card, Daddy will kill me!" *Don't laugh,* I commanded myself at the thought of my dad — an accountant who is basically Mr. Never-put-anything-on-a-credit-card — letting me have my own Visa.

"Adrianna, that is what you always say, and he *never* minds!" Lindsay replied. "Still, I think that jacket is a little —" She waved her hand.

"Last season?" I volunteered for her.

"Exactly!" Lindsay turned to the saleslady. "Well, thank you so much, you've been a dear!"

"Would you like to be on our mailing list?" she asked hopefully.

"Oh, I already *am,*" Lindsay assured her. "Jean-Paul and I both are, for the Beverly Hills store. But perhaps we'll pop in the next time we're in town! Ciao!"

"Thanks *ever* so!" I added, slipping the jacket back into place and scuttling after Lindsay.

We waited until we had safely turned the corner before completely losing it. "Daddy's credit card!" Lindsay shrieked. She was laughing so hard her eyes were watering.

"And *what* was that accent?" I shot back, giggling madly. " 'You've been a dear!' " I mimicked.

"Eh, she deserved it." Lindsay wiped her eyes.

"Okay," I said. "So much for our reconnaissance mission. Next time, I get to pick the store."

"Fair enough," Lindsay agreed. "So — where to?"

"Didn't your sisters say we should check out Burn?" I asked. It was a trendy shop — half of the high school kids bought their clothes there.

Lindsay grinned. "Let's hit it."

The music was pulsing so loudly I could feel it in my chest, like a second heartbeat. Burn was cool all right. Super-cool. Trendy girls stood at nearby racks, scooping up jeans and teeny tiny miniskirts like they were wads of cash dumped from the ceiling. The funny thing was that most of the girls were already wearing outfits just like the ones they were cooing over.

Still, they looked like teenage rock stars, and — even in my Tracy Sweet Special — I was feeling like a fake.

"I like this belt," I said, pulling a cool black leather number from the rack. "It would look good with jeans."

Lindsay grabbed the belt out of my hands. "Nick, that's a skirt," she said, placing it back on the rack.

I glanced at the rest of the store. "Man, they have a huge underwear section."

Lindsay cleared her throat. "I'm not sure that's underwear. I mean, I think they're just clothes."

"Oh." I blushed a little, feeling like a five-year-old.

"Well, okay — so these clothes aren't our usual style," Lindsay said.

"Not by a long shot," I agreed, thinking about my soccer jerseys. They didn't have anything remotely like that in this store.

"But that's the point, isn't it?" Lindsay looked at me. She scrunched up her mouth, like she does when she's thinking. "I mean, we're going for a new style, right? Maybe we should try a few things and see how they look."

I shrugged. "Okay."

We split up to poke around a little. I pulled out a turquoise V-neck T-shirt that didn't seem too flashy. Then I pulled out a pair of skinny-looking jeans. Hey — at least they were jeans, right?

I met Lindsay by a rack of caps. She was holding up an orange dress with a short skirt, a scoop neck, and short sleeves. "What do you think?"

"Has potential," I told her, and the two of us headed for the dressing room.

The stalls were lined with stickers and plastered with concert posters — all bands I'd never heard of. *Who are the Skanky Squirrels?* I wondered as I attempted to shimmy into the jeans. And another weird thing about the dressing room — there was no mirror. I had to step outside to see myself.

Ugh.

The jeans didn't want to close. The label had said that they were my size, but . . . *Well, maybe they're supposed to be tight,* I reasoned. I sucked it in and managed to squeeze the button closed and zip them up. Talk about uncomfortable. These things were for people who didn't need to breathe.

Even over the pulsing music, I heard Lindsay give a surprised giggle from the stall next to mine.

"Everything okay?"

"I'll show you my outfit if you show me yours," Lindsay said with a smile in her voice.

"Sure." I pulled on the shirt and opened the door.

Peeking out, Lindsay gave me the once over and stopped. "Wow, Nick — that's a new look for you."

Turning, I caught my reflection in the mirror. Whoa. The T-shirt was cut low — *way* low. I yanked it up, and the bottom exposed my midriff. *Great.*

"The jeans look good," Lindsay said.

"Yeah, but they're cutting off the circulation to my legs," I told her. "But your dress looks nice." It was true. The orange color looked surprisingly good on her, and the dress was a little short, but not something she could get sent home for.

She smiled mischievously. “You think so?” she asked, giving a slow twirl.

I snorted with laughter. The dress had no back! “Just don’t sit near the air vent in math,” I told her. “You’ll catch a cold.”

“Oh, yeah, I can just imagine what the Block would have to say about this outfit.” Lindsay giggled. The Block was our math teacher — Henrietta Blockson. She was a very *solid* woman, and she always wore either black or gray. “Lindsay, dear,” Lindsay said in the Block’s trademark nasal whine, “don’t you think that dress is a little *much*?” The Block always thought things were a little *much*.

I cracked up.

“It’s an unexpected look, all right.” I peered in the mirror again, grinning at the girl in the low-cut outfit. “I guess this is one way to get Ben’s attention.”

“Yeah,” Lindsay agreed. “He’ll take one look at you and think you’ve gone completely nuts.”

“These outfits are a little *too* not us,” I said.

“Please — we’d have to get brain transplants to wear them,” Lindsay agreed.

“Okay.” I sighed. “I am declaring this little experiment with Burn fashion officially over.”

"On to the next store," Lindsay said brightly. "Cheer up," she added, poking me in the shoulder. "Hey — at least we're figuring out what we don't want to wear, right? That's just as good as figuring out what we do want."

"Good point." I felt a little better as I headed back into my stall to remove the Torture Jeans. Lindsay was right. So we'd had a couple of misses. That just meant we were due for a hit!

"My feet are killing me," Lindsay griped as she dipped a white plastic spoon into a cup of chocolate fudge frozen yogurt. We had decided to take a break at the food court. "How many miles of mall do you think we've walked in the past two hours?"

"Feels like a hundred," I said, flexing my toes. It was kind of weird to think that I had spent every afternoon this week running at basketball practice — but somehow that didn't seem nearly as tiring as a couple of hours at the mall. "Can we officially give up now?"

"I think we may have to." Lindsay sounded kind of dejected. "We're supposed to meet your mom in forty-five minutes, and we haven't found a single thing."

"You bought that lip gloss," I reminded her.

"We haven't found anything to *wear,*" she elaborated.

I sighed. After Burn, we had cruised the mall, hitting store after store. First, there was the Corral. But neither one of us was into huge belt buckles and denim on denim, so we moved on. Next up was Faerie, where they sold gargoyles and black velvet capes. I was sort of tempted by the black glitter nail polish, but when Lindsay said that it would make me look cool, "in a vampire way," I decided against it. Then there was Ports of Call (ten thousand Indian skirts with sequins at the hem), Sugar's (everything pink), and F. J. Hammersmith (too blah). I was starting to feel a little like Goldilocks. But without the just-right porridge.

"We could go back to F. J. Hammersmith," I said, without enthusiasm. At least the clothes there were practical — if boring.

Lindsay shook her head, licking her spoon. "We want something that expresses our personalities," she said. "Not just nice clothes, you know?"

"I know." I dug into my vanilla with peanut butter sauce. *Why isn't finding something to wear as easy as picking out your favorite flavor?* I wondered.

"Don't look up," Lindsay murmured suddenly, staring into her frozen yogurt, and so — of course — I looked up.

Shoot. Why don't I ever listen to my best friend? I wondered as my eyes caught Hannah's. Her lips twitched over to one side in a snarky smile, and she sidled over to our table. Two of her cronies — Abby Smith and DeLinda Trainor — trailed behind her.

"Hello, Nick," Hannah said. "Kind of surprising to see you here."

"Hi," I said, smiling at Abby and DeLinda. They didn't see me, though. They were staring off at the Golden Panda, whispering about what to order.

"Hi, Hannah," Lindsay piped up.

Hannah just nodded at her. Sometimes it's hard to believe how obnoxious she can be. I don't think that she has ever said hello to Lindsay, even though we've all been in classes together for the past four years. Lindsay always says hi to her, though. I think she just does it to annoy Hannah, actually.

"Doing a little shopping?" Hannah asked, tossing her long hair over one shoulder. She looked perfect, as usual — a purple fitted T-shirt and super-dark jeans that didn't seem to be cutting off her blood flow. *How does she do it?* I wondered. "I thought you only bought things from The Athlete's Foot."

Abby giggled and DeLinda punched her in the arm. I couldn't help wondering where DeLinda got her cool green wrap skirt. It was just the kind of thing I was looking for. And Abby had on really great embroidered shoes that went with her pink cropped pants. I guess I was distracted by their clothes, because I heard myself say, "I only buy my *cleats* at The Athlete's Foot. They have good deals."

Now DeLinda gave a snort and Abby had to punch her.

Lindsay shook her head and took another bite of her frozen yogurt.

"Try to remember not to wear cleats to the party, Nick," Hannah said with a smirk. "It marks up the floor." Laughing, she and her two cronies pranced away.

I watched them walk toward the Golden Panda. *They even* walk *differently than I do,* I thought. *I sort of clump along, but they float. . . .*

Suddenly, I felt eyes boring into my skull. Looking over, I saw Lindsay staring at me. "What?" I asked.

"'They have great deals on cleats'?" Lindsay quoted. "That was your comeback?"

I winced. "That's not *exactly* what I said."

"What kind of a comeback is that?" she demanded.

"Okay, okay, it was lame," I admitted. "Lame, but true."

"Who cares if it's true?" Lindsay shot back. "That's not the point!"

"There's a point?"

"Yes, Nick, there's a point." Lindsay huffed and sat back in her chair. "If you want to beat Hannah at her own game, then you have to *play* Hannah's game."

I let a spoonful of gooey peanut butter sauce melt on my tongue, then said, "I'm not following you."

Lindsay sighed. "It's not just about clothes, Nick. It's about attitude."

"Yeah." I glanced over at the giggling trio, who were now eating egg rolls and flirting with a group of good-looking boys who had descended to a table next to theirs. Hannah cocked one shoulder easily and dipped her egg roll into some sauce, taking a delicate bite. Then she said something that made the boys crack up. "Yeah, I noticed," I said.

"It's about how you walk, how you talk, what you say — not just what you wear, but how you wear it," Lindsay went on. "Even if we manage to get some clothes, you're going to need some practice."

"Practice?"

"You can't just walk into Hannah's party next week and expect to be queen of the place," Lindsay explained. "Hannah is used to being the queen. If you want Ben to talk to you and not her, you're going to have to learn how to make guys listen."

I thought it over. What Lindsay said had the ring of truth. "But how?"

Lindsay leaned forward. "Oh, crud — look, I just dripped chocolate frozen yogurt on Stacy's dress!" She stuck her paper napkin in her glass of water and dabbed at the stain. "Okay, I think it's coming out. Does this look like it's coming out?"

"It's coming out," I told her.

"Really? Because she'll totally kill me —"

"Lindsay, it's coming out," I told her. "It's just dark because of the water." I didn't mean to sound impatient, but I wanted to hear more about this practice idea. An image of Ben was floating through my mind like a Christmas sugarplum vision.

"Okay. Okay — what was I saying?" She frowned at the stain, still dabbing at it.

"I need practice —"

"Right! Okay, my cousin's bar mitzvah is tonight, and he's having a reception tomorrow afternoon," Lindsay said. "David Silver. It'll be a huge party. If you come along, you can practice chatting with a few guys."

I thought it over. "What if I make an idiot of myself?" I asked.

"Then you never have to see any of them again,"

Lindsay said, tossing her napkin into a nearby trash can. *Two points — she should join the basketball team,* I thought. "They live on the other side of town."

"Well . . ." I sighed. Going to a party full of people I didn't know wasn't exactly my idea of fun. "You'll be there, right?"

"Right. I'll have your back."

"Okay," I said at last. "Okay . . . but we still don't have anything to wear."

"Tell me about it." Lindsay poked at the stain on her lap, then gave up. "I can't even look at this anymore," she said in disgust, frowning at the guilty cup of chocolate frozen yogurt. "You've stained my sister's dress, and I hate you, chocolate yogurt!" Standing, she grabbed the dish and carried it to the garbage. She stood there a moment, perfectly still. "Nick!"

"What?"

"Look!" Lindsay pointed to a boutique right across the way. The sign read FUCHSIA FLOWER. Right below was a banner: GRAND OPENING SALE!

We hurried over to take a closer look. In the window were two mannequins. One had on a red dress with a fun print of black poodles all over it. It wrapped around in a cool way. The other had on black cropped pants and a swingy pink-and-yellow print top that was fitted at the top and flowy on the bottom.

Lindsay and I looked at each other. “Cool!” we said in unison.

Lindsay gestured toward the entrance. “Shall we?” she asked.

I grinned at her. “We shall!” It looked like Goldilocks had finally found the just-right porridge!

DAY FOUR

SUNDAY

Chat Up Your Crush!

How to Get Him Talking!

Ask questions! Every guy's favorite topic is HIMSELF, so ask and you shall receive — info! Find out his favorite movies, sports stars, or food — he'll probably tell you more than you want to know, and you'll have material for *hours* of convo!

★★★

"Who do you think this looks good on?" Lindsay asked as she pointed to a palette of vibrant purple blush.

"Clowns," I said, and Lindsay giggled, earning a slight frown from the tall, imposing-looking woman behind the counter. It was Sunday morning, and we were standing in Charlie's, which has the best selection of makeup in town. For some reason, it's located in a strip mall five blocks from my house, between a dentist's office and a dog-grooming studio. Not exactly the glamour capital of the world — but convenient. Plus, Tracy told us that they let you try stuff out. Which is what we needed to do, since I'm fully makeup-impaired, and Lindsay knows how to do Frankenstein, but hasn't exactly mastered the easy-breezy all-natural look yet.

"Actually," the tall woman said to me, "someone with your coloring could pull this off."

I grimaced. "I don't think I'm brave enough for a color like that."

"It doesn't go on as purple as it looks," the woman said. "Do you want to try it?"

I glanced over at Lindsay, who pursed her lips dubiously. It was obvious that she thought this woman had no idea what she was talking about. Still, I was feeling kind of adventurous, so I heard myself say, "Sure. Why not?"

The woman pulled out an oversized brush and dabbed it against the purple. Her gray hair was swept up in a neat bun, and she was wearing a flowing purple dress. She had on a ton of makeup — when she leaned close, I counted four different eyeshadow colors on her lids — which made sense, given her job. "Do you have Mediterranean blood?"

she asked as she swept the brush gently against my cheek.

"My mom is Italian," I said, and she nodded.

"Brunette people look great in bold colors. This will really bring out your eyes." She pursed her lips, then pulled a pink eye shadow off of the rack. "This will give you a little sparkle, open you up. I hope you don't mind?"

"Oh, go nuts," I told her, figuring I could wash it all off later.

Beside me, Lindsay pulled out a hot pink lipstick.

"Put that down, honey," the woman said. "That's not for you."

Lindsay hesitated. "My sister said that I should go for some bright lipstick."

She rolled her eyes. "Who are you going to trust — your sister, or Charlie?"

"*You're* Charlie?" Lindsay said. "*The* Charlie, who owns this store?"

"Sure am." Charlie used a Q-tip to brush some eye shadow across my lids, then turned to frown at the lipstick selection. "Passion flower, where did you go?" she muttered. "Where are you when I want you?"

"I heard that you used to do the makeup for the

Total Teen beauty spreads," Lindsay said, leaning against the glass counter.

"Oh, sure, I was a makeup artist and stylist for years," Charlie told her. "There you are!" She pulled a lipstick out of the display and turned to smile at Lindsay. "Just because I'm a little older than you doesn't mean I don't know what I'm doing."

"I never would have thought that!" Lindsay insisted, which made me laugh a little, because I knew that she had been thinking that very thing.

"What kind of mascara are you using?" Charlie asked me. "Because I think you should go for dark brown."

"I don't use any mascara," I told her. "I don't usually wear makeup."

"Darling!" Charlie exclaimed. "So, what's the occasion?"

"We're going to a party later," I told her. "Lindsay and I — this is Lindsay, by the way, and I'm Nick."

Charlie nodded. "Nice to meet you."

"Same here. Anyway, we're going to a party, and we have outfits, but we kind of need a crash course beauty lesson."

"So this is a one-day affair?" Charlie said. "You shouldn't have to buy a lot of makeup if you're never going to use it again."

"Oh, no, we're giving ourselves total makeovers,"

Lindsay announced. "Nick has a mad crush on this guy, and she's trying to get his attention."

"Lindsay!" I shrieked.

Charlie's face softened, and she blinked dreamily. "Ah, young love," she said, sighing. "Is he very handsome?" she asked me.

I felt myself blush.

"Very," Lindsay piped up.

Charlie pulled out a sheet of paper with a face printed on it. "I'll show you how to do everything," she said, swiping the blush she had used onto the paper face and making a note by it. "You can take this home, so you can see what we did here. I'll do one for you, too," she told Lindsay.

Wincing slightly, Lindsay glanced at a list of prices posted on the makeup counter. BEAUTY LESSON WITH PROFESSIONAL MAKEUP ARTIST: $50. "Um . . . we don't have a lot of money," Lindsay said.

Reaching out, Charlie flipped down the sign. "Sunday morning special," she said as she scribbled madly on the paper face. "No charge. Now, for the mascara — most people will tell you to spend a lot on an expensive brand, but I'm here to tell you that the cheap stuff works just as well. What you want to do is pick the colors using the expensive brands, because they have a bigger selection, then match them as well as you can with the things that cost a third of the price." She yanked something off the wall and ripped it out of the packaging to apply some to my lashes. "Look at the ceiling," she said, and I did. "Now blink into the brush. We'll just do the top lashes for you — it's subtler. I'm thinking we need something simple and flirty for every day."

"Flirty is key," Lindsay agreed.

"But for you — maybe something a little more dramatic," Charlie suggested. "I'm thinking apricot, with a little sparkle. There's something theatrical about you."

"She's in the drama club," I volunteered.

"That explains it," Charlie said, nodding. "There. Look at yourself." She angled a mirror toward me, so that I could see my face.

"Wow — you can hardly even tell I'm wearing any makeup," I said.

"Except that your eyes . . ." Lindsay's voice trailed off.

"Yeah." I knew what she meant. I didn't look like regular old me. I looked like somebody needed to put a "new-and-improved" sticker on my forehead. Even so, Charlie had been right. That purple blush didn't look purple on my face; it looked totally natural.

"That blush is expensive," Charlie said, "and it's

the one thing you won't find for cheap. I'll give you a couple of free samples to start."

"Thank you!" I said, breathlessly. Wow. I couldn't believe our luck.

Charlie winked as she pulled out a small shopping basket and tossed a handful of samples inside. "Anything for love," she said. "But you have to promise to come back and tell me if you get the boy."

I crossed my heart. "Swear."

"And you," Charlie said to Lindsay. "Something tells me there's a boy in the picture for you, too, am I right?"

Lindsay blushed, mashing her lips together. She turned bright red, and I couldn't help wondering what makeup colors would go with that look.

"Not ready to say who it is." Charlie nodded. "But I expect you to come by and tell me if it works out, all right? Promise?"

Lindsay nodded. "Promise," she squeaked.

I lifted my eyebrows. *That's right,* I thought, *I'd completely forgotten that Lindsay had a secret crush. Who is it?* I made a mental note to bug her about it later.

"All right, then." Charlie bustled through the store, pulling out products and tossing them into our basket. "The least expensive thing on the market," she said as she put in a lipstick. "And the best.

Here's that mascara you tried on. And of course you need makeup remover. Be sure to take all of it off every night, or your skin will pay the price. Okay, let's ring you up."

By the time we left, Lindsay and I had fabulous faces and bags full of everything we'd need to make ourselves look great at the bar mitzvah. Plus, we paid way less than we thought we'd have to. Charlie had given us more free samples than we knew what to do with. She even threw in some perfume.

"I think I'm ready for my close-up," I told Lindsay as we headed toward my house.

Lindsay nodded. "It's time for the dress rehearsal."

Now all I had to do was learn my lines.

Lindsay held up a flash card. "Jock," she read.

"Ask him what sports he's into," I told her.

"Yep!" Lindsay flipped to the next flash card. "Prep."

"What's your favorite book?"

"Right. Or you could ask about his favorite author. Great." Lindsay smiled. "You're going to be the smoothest girl at the party!"

I was sitting cross-legged on my bed, while Lindsay was perched in my red comfy chair that sits by the window. That's where I do most of my reading, curled up next to the arm. Lindsay was wearing brown Mary Janes and a brown minidress with a burnt-orange lace piece that fit over the top. With her red hair, she looked like an autumn leaf. I had on a cool knee-length cotton knit skirt that looked like it wrapped around, but really just had three layers. It was black, and I was wearing it with a fuchsia V-neck top edged in lace. And, of course, we each had on our Perfect Face, courtesy of Charlie.

Lindsay checked her watch. "I think my mom will be here soon."

I fiddled with the jeweled mini-barrette in my hair. "Are you sure it's okay if I come along?"

"Don't touch it," Lindsay commanded, eyeing my barrette. "You'll pull it out. My aunt said I could bring a friend, so relax. Besides, it's going to be a huge party. There will be family members there who I've never even met, so it's not like you'll stick out or anything. Okay." She flipped up the next flash card. "No particular type."

"I want to see a movie this weekend — have you seen anything good lately?" I recited. I felt like I was cramming for a Spanish test. The flash cards had been Lindsay's idea. She put them together after reading an article about how to talk to guys in

Young Woman, and she was *extremely* proud of them.

"And what if he hasn't?" Lindsay prompted.

I squeezed my eyes shut. "Ask him how he knows the host — David."

"Right!" She grinned. "You're a natural."

I scooted off of my bed and walked over to peer at myself in the mirror. "I don't feel like a natural," I said uncertainly. "Are you sure I look okay?"

"You look great!" Lindsay said. "What are you worried about? Your hair is gorgeous."

"I don't know about these shoes," I confessed, looking down at the pointy-toed heels I was wearing. The heel was low, but that wasn't helping much. "I can hardly walk."

"We'll probably be sitting the whole time," Lindsay promised.

"And this shirt is kind of tight." I tried pulling it away from my waist, but it snapped back into place. "It's squeezing me."

"Look, I can't bend over in this thing," Lindsay confessed, gesturing toward her dress. "But who cares? That's not the point."

Just then, my door flew open and Alex burst in, saying, "Lindsay, your mo —"

That's as far as he got: "your mo." Because when he saw us, his voice ceased functioning. He looked at me first and his jaw dropped, but when his eyes landed on Lindsay, he positively gaped. His eyes bugged out of his head, froglike, and his lips parted and closed, parted and closed, but no sound came out.

Lindsay giggled, blushing.

Poor Alex. I felt kind of bad for him, standing there in a pair of baggy jeans and a ratty old T-shirt while we were looking so good. I guess Lindsay caught him off guard. "Lindsay's mom is here?"

Alex blinked at me, like he was waking up from a dream. "What?"

"Did you come up here to tell us that Lindsay's mom is here?" I repeated, a little more slowly this time.

"What? Oh — yeah! She's — uh —" Alex jerked his thumb behind him, then twisted, retreating halfway out the door. "She's — uh — she —"

"She's waiting for us?" I guessed.

Alex pointed at me. "That." He nodded, then looked at Lindsay again, wide-eyed, cleared his throat, and scurried away.

Lindsay and I looked at each other in surprise, then cracked up.

"I guess the outfits are working!" Lindsay said happily, picking up her bag. It was brown suede, and had cool fringe hanging from it.

"Maybe a little *too* well," I said. I mean, it isn't easy to make my brother speechless — I can tell you that for a fact.

"Too well? Nicolette Spicer," Lindsay said as we hurried out the door to meet her mother, "you know there is no such thing."

"You didn't tell me that we were going to the Wilcox Hotel," I whispered to Lindsay as her dad handed the car keys to the valet. The Wilcox is the fanciest hotel in the city. I'd never even been inside.

"Oh. Well, we're going to the Wilcox," Lindsay said.

"David's family is loaded," Tracy put in.

"*Filthy* rich," Stacy agreed, tossing her curly hair.

"Girls," Lindsay's mom, Andrea, cast a warning glance at her daughters. "It's rude to talk about people's money."

Tracy cocked a perfectly plucked eyebrow as we walked into the black marble entrance. "Rude, but true," she said, eyeing a flower arrangement that was bigger than me. Birds-of-paradise and other exotic blooms burst out of a huge vase decorated with ceramic ferns. Palm trees and other lush greenery filled the lobby, and there was a large waterfall that burbled away, the water flowing over black rocks, at the center of the room. Overhead, a glass ceiling lit the space with a beautiful, natural glow. The whole effect was kind of like the world's fanciest man-made tropical rain forest.

"We're in the Hamilton Room," Lindsay's dad said, glancing at the invitation. He led us through the reception area and into an enormous room. One wall was lined with floor-to-ceiling windows, trimmed in hunter green curtains. Each table was topped with small ferns and red tropical flowers. A band was on a platform at one end, performing "Pretty Woman," and a few people had already stepped onto the dance floor. It was just beautiful.

A short woman who was about as wide as she was tall beamed at us from beneath a helmet of perfectly coiffed gray hair. "Darlings!" she cried the minute she laid eyes on us. "Robert, you gorgeous man — look at your beautiful family! Tracy, I love that red dress, darling. Look, I'm in red, too — everyone will think we planned our outfits. And Stacy, dear, you look like a movie star! And who is this? Why, I haven't seen Lindsay in ages! Come give me a kiss, you sweet thing!"

"Hi, Great-aunt Rita," Lindsay said, giving the woman a peck on the cheek.

Great-aunt Rita wrapped her in a huge hug,

then turned to me. "And who is this gorgeous, gorgeous girl?"

"My best friend, Nick." Lindsay smiled, and I smiled, too. In fact, everyone was smiling. Great-aunt Rita's enthusiasm was infectious.

"Well, aren't you all a picture — simply a *picture*! Now, girls, you'll be at table D. Robert and Andrea, come this way, darlings — you're sitting with me!"

"You know, you two are looking . . ." Tracy searched for the right word as we made our way to table D. ". . . better," she finished.

"Really?" Lindsay looked over at Stacy for confirmation.

"Don't talk to me," Stacy said. She was still mad about the chocolate stain on her pink dress. "But yes, really. Much better."

I was so surprised to hear Stacy's compliment that I stumbled a little in my new shoes. I looked around to see if anyone noticed that I'd tripped, and that was when I saw Ben, sitting over at a table full of guys — and tripped again.

"Are you okay?" Lindsay asked, catching my elbow to keep me from falling.

"Ben's here," I whispered as I slid into my chair. Finally — sitting. *I am not getting up ever again,* I swore silently.

"He is?" Lindsay craned her neck. "Oh, you're right! Hey, Ben!" she called, waving.

I grabbed her hand. "What are you doing?" I hissed. "I don't want to see him yet!"

But it was too late. He'd seen us. He was getting out of his chair. . . .

"What do you mean?" Lindsay demanded. "You look great! This is perfect!"

"But this is supposed to be *practice*!" I pointed out.

"Oh, right," Lindsay said. "Well, too late!"

"Look, there's Rachel," Tracy said to Stacy. "Let's say hi. See you two later."

"Good luuuuck," Stacy singsonged at me, giving Ben a grin as he walked up to the table. He was wearing a blue shirt and a striped tie, with olive green pants. He looked, if possible, even cuter than usual.

"Well, if it isn't Lindsay Sweet and Drink-spilling Girl," Ben said as he sat down in Tracy's chair. He smiled at me. "Nick, right?"

I actually had to think about that for a minute. My name sounded different when he said it. Better. "Right," I said at last.

Lindsay looked at me, and I struggled to remember my conversation starters but came up completely blank. They flew straight out of my brain — every single one.

Luckily, my best friend seemed to grasp the situation and jumped in. "So Ben, how do you know David?"

"We went to school together last year. We were in the same science class," Ben explained. "How do you know him?"

"We're cousins," Lindsay said.

"And you know David because of Lindsay?" Ben asked me.

I'd actually never met David, but this explanation was close enough to the truth for me, so I said, "Yep."

And we sat there. Lindsay cleared her throat and kicked me under the table. It didn't make me think of anything to say.

"Well," Ben said after a moment. "I should get back to David. He's actually pretty miserable right now."

"Really?" I asked. "Why? It looks like a great party."

"He wanted something a lot more low-key to celebrate getting bar mitzvahed," Ben explained. "He was thinking ten guys going to play laser tag. But his mother and his Great-aunt Rita got together and . . ."

"... he ended up with the social event of the century at the Wilcox," I finished for him.

A smile ticked up at the corner of Ben's mouth. "Something like that."

"Well, maybe we'll see you on the dance floor later," Lindsay suggested.

Ben winced. "I don't really dance," he admitted. Then he walked away.

"Well, that was awkward," I said, once he was out of earshot. Which wasn't that long, since the band was now playing a rousing rendition of "Disco Inferno."

"You've got to relax," Lindsay said, punching my shoulder lightly. "Get into character. You're a flirt! A diva! You're gorgeous and you know it!"

"I am?"

"Sure — just do a little acting," Lindsay said. "Don't think so much. Just remember that guys like to talk about themselves, okay?"

"Excuse me, is this table D?"

Looking up, I saw that a cute boy with curly blond hair was standing at the chair next to mine.

"I'm supposed to be at table D," he explained.

"You found it!" Lindsay chirped, stepping lightly on my toe.

Okay — a new test subject, I thought as he sat down beside me. *And he's even kind of cute. Perfect.*

"I'm Nicolette," I told him, "and this is Lindsay."

"Greg Fisher," the cute boy said with a huge smile. "Haven't I seen you two around? Don't you go to Garfield Middle?"

"Yeah," I told him. "We're in sixth grade."

"I'm in eighth," he said a little self-importantly, like being an eighth grader was a huge accomplishment.

Well, whatever. He was just Practice Boy. *Okay,* I thought, sizing him up. *He looks a little jockish.* "Do you play any sports?" I asked.

"Wrestling," Greg said. "It's a great sport, and I can't figure out why more people don't come to watch us compete. Do you know we have the best record in the city? Most people at Garfield have no idea. Which is really sad, because it's a classic, classic sport. Greco-Roman — people have been doing it for centuries." And then he launched into an explanation of weight classes and wrestling techniques that lasted through the entire salad course.

This is working great! I thought as he continued to talk. *I mean, sure — it's kind of boring — but whatever!* Finally, he ran out of steam.

"Seen any good movies lately?" I asked him.

"Oh, yeah — have you seen *Kung Fu Kangaroo*?

It's hilarious! There's this great scene where the kangaroo, okay, there's this diamond thief, right? And he's got a sack full of diamonds. . . ."

I nodded as if I had some idea what he was talking about, and he continued to tell me the plot of the entire movie. All I had to do was nod my head and say, "That sounds really funny," every few minutes, and he just kept on going.

"You should definitely see it," he said finally.

Of course, I didn't need to see it, given that he had just told me everything about it, but I just said, "It sounds really interesting."

Beside me, Lindsay gave a little snort and dug into her chicken.

"Oh, hey!" Greg said suddenly. "They're playing that song! Oh, this is so great — we have to go dance to it!" He grabbed my hand.

I was surprised and flattered. *He wants to dance? With me? That magazine is a genius!* I thought. "What song?"

"It's the hora," Lindsay said, scooting her chair back. "Everyone dances in a circle. It's really fun — let's go!"

Sure enough, the dance floor was packed, and people were dancing around in a circle. Even Ben was there, on the far side of the floor. For someone who doesn't dance, he was doing a good job. There seemed to be steps involved, but I thought maybe I could fake it, with a little hopping.

"Join us, dearies!" Great-aunt Rita gestured wildly, grabbing Lindsay by the hand. "Oh, isn't it delightful? Isn't this *fun*?"

Lindsay grabbed my right hand, and Greg grabbed my left, and in the next moment, I was swept into the swirling dance. I clomped after Lindsay, but I'd only taken about three steps when my shoe fell off, and I toppled over. Face-first.

Laughing, Greg swirled out of the way, but a tall man with enormous feet tripped over my leg with an "Oof!"

"Uncle Ephraim, what are you doing?" someone called, and soon the line of dancers was crashing into each other.

"Omigosh, Nick, are you okay?" Lindsay cried. The momentum had momentarily swept her away, but she fought her way back to help me.

"Oh, dear. Darling, are you hurt?" Great-aunt Rita was right behind her.

"I'm okay," I said, reaching out for the first hand that came my way. I was blushing madly, and my ankle felt a little sore, as if I had twisted it.

"Are you sure?" asked a familiar voice, and I looked up into a pair of gorgeous brown eyes. Ben.

He was the one who had helped me up, and I was still holding his hand. "I'm fine," I said. His fingers were warm.

He smiled. "You've sure got some original moves," he joked.

"Oh, man! That was *classic*!" Greg howled, practically holding his sides.

I felt my face burning madly. *Why do I have to be such an oaf whenever Ben is around?* I thought, silently cursing myself. I was so furious at my own clumsiness that tears sprang into my eyes, which made me even madder. I'm not a big crier, but there I was, about to start bawling at David Silver's bar mitzvah.

"Are you sure you're okay?" Ben asked gently.

Lindsay seemed to know exactly how I was feeling, because she grabbed my arm and started to steer me away. "She's great! We're just going to the ladies' room to clean up. Back in a jiff! Go ahead and dance the hora, everyone!" And she half-steered, half-shoved me out of there.

"It's okay," she whispered, wrapping her arm around me as we ducked down the hall. "It's okay. It's not as bad as you think."

"You are such a liar," I told her.

"I know," Lindsay admitted, giving me a gentle squeeze.

I sighed. "You're a good friend, Lindsay Sweet."

"I know that, too," she said as she led me into the bathroom. "But look on the bright side — our experiment totally worked. Greg Fisher thinks you're great! So you totally know how to talk to guys. And Ben will have forgotten all about this by Hannah's party next weekend."

"You really think so?" I asked hopefully.

"Um, no," Lindsay admitted. "But you sure got his attention."

"Yeah," I said with a sigh. "And he said it himself — I've sure got original moves."

DAY FIVE

MONDAY

HOROSCOPE

Aries (March 20–April 21)

Crossed wires will make you feel like your world has turned upside down and inside out! Just remember — you're not crazy. Everyone else is.

"Would you get out of there?" Alex banged on the bathroom door twice, then gave it an extra-hard thump for good measure. "I have to take a shower!"

"I'm almost done!" I ran my hands through my hair. For some reason, I couldn't make it do the funky spiky poufy thing that both Lindsay and Tracy had made look so simple. I'd spent thirty minutes and used half a container of my special styling paste, and now my head looked lopsided. Not to mention the twenty minutes attempting to get my mascara to go on without glopping. And I'd still have to try to put on some blush and eyeshadow in the girls' room before first period. If I tried to wear it out of the house, I knew my mom would freak. *This makeover stuff is work,* I decided. *I'll have to get up earlier tomorrow.*

"You've been in there for forty-five minutes!" Alex cried, like overspending my bathroom time was an outrage against humanity. *Thud!* That sounded like a kick.

"Jeez, all right, all right," I grumbled, shoving the styling paste back into the medicine cabinet. I knew I'd better get out of there before Alex busted down the door, so I clipped a sparkly barrette into my bangs and let him in. "It's all yours."

"Why are you so dressed up?" Alex demanded. He was sporting a serious case of bed-head, and his eyes were bugged out. In his ratty old plaid pajamas, he looked kind of demented.

I peered down at my outfit — a green dress with a ruffle at the bottom and an embroidered jacket. I was wearing comfortable shoes, though — a pair of flats. No more heels for me. "I'm not dressed up."

Alex pointed at my dress. "What do you call that?"

"A dress."

"Oh, and you don't call that dressed up?" Alex demanded. "You? *You,* who thought it was perfectly appropriate to wear a sweatshirt with a hole in the armpit to Mom's cousin Barbara's wedding?"

"Nobody could see the hole!" I pointed out. "Besides, Mom made me change."

"What did I forget?" Alex ran his fingers through his bangs, which only made them stick out to the side in an even crazier way. "Picture day? It is, isn't it?"

"Alex, it was picture day last month, remember?" I told him. "I swear, I'm just dressed, not dressed up." *Jeez, can't a girl look nice without her own brother freaking out?*

Alex narrowed his green eyes and slung his towel over his shoulder. "Forty-five minutes in the bathroom and a dress," he said suspiciously. "What are you trying to pull?"

"Alex!" Dad called. "Nick! You're going to miss breakfast if you don't get a move on!"

"Be right down!" I shouted.

"Is some kind of special project due?" Alex asked, like he was a lawyer cross-examining me. "Do we have to make a presentation? The science fair isn't for months. . . ."

"There's nothing."

"Why won't you just tell me?"

"There's nothing — I swear!"

"Oh, yeah — right!"

"Sometimes I find it hard to believe that we're twins," I told him, turning toward the stairs.

"That's how I know what you're thinking, sister!" Alex called as he backed into the bathroom. "Well, you're not going to make me look like an idiot! I'm going to shower like the wind, and then *I'm* going to look good!"

"Okay, nutburger!" I shouted as Alex slammed the bathroom door closed.

"Oh, Nick, don't you look pretty!" Mom said as I walked into the kitchen. She was wearing the red blouse she had bought at the mall tucked into a brown skirt. The outfit looked just right on her.

Dad put a glass of orange juice at my place. "Something special at school today, Nick?" he asked as I sat down at the breakfast table.

I sighed. I was starting to realize that this makeover was a little more drastic than I had thought. "Nothing special. I just wanted to wear my new clothes."

Mom reached out and fluffed my hair a little. "There," she said. "You look gorgeous."

"Thanks, Mom." I bit into my toast. I knew one thing for sure — being gorgeous ain't easy.

* * *

"Oh, wow!" Carla was the first person who spotted me when I walked out of the girls' room. My face had been "re-Charlified." I knew it wasn't perfect, but it was as good as I could get it. "Nick, you look fantastic!"

"Outta sight!" Josie added. She's on a mission to bring back expressions from the seventies, by the way. "What's the occasion?"

"Monday," I said as I headed to my locker. It was kind of a weird feeling — having so many people comment on how I looked. I felt like I had a big neon arrow over my head or something.

"Hi, Nick!"

Turning, I saw Hannah leaning against the locker beside mine. She looked perfect as usual, in a blue corduroy miniskirt and soft green sweater. She gave me an up-and-down look, smirking. "Looks like you've got a hot date."

I don't know how she managed it, but that look wiped away the pretty vibes I'd been feeling all morning and made me feel like an idiot. Blushing, I said, "Yeah, right."

"Don't be embarrassed — the whole school is talking about it." Hannah tucked a lock of blond hair behind her ear.

I pulled my thick social studies book out of my locker. "Talking about what?"

"You and Greg Fisher, silly," Hannah said. "See you later, Nick!" And then she walked away, before I had a chance to say anything.

Okay, that was totally weird, I thought as I slammed my locker and spun the combination on my lock. Turning, I nearly ran right into Lindsay.

"What's this about Greg Fisher?" she demanded.

I nearly jumped out of my skin. "What?"

"Ellie Jackson just told me that you and Greg are going out! She said that it's all over school! Why didn't you mention it, Nick? I can't believe I had to hear it from *Ellie,* of all people!" When Lindsay said the name "Ellie," she sounded like a cat with a hairball, like the letters were stuck in her throat. Not that there's anything wrong with Ellie, exactly. It's just that she's one of those girls who are so nice they make you want to barf.

"It's not true!" I insisted. "I barely even know Greg!"

Lindsay looked surprised. "Seriously?"

"Like I'd tell Ellie Jackson something like that before I told you." I rolled my eyes. "Get real!"

"So wait — why are you so dressed up?" Lindsay asked, eyeing my outfit.

"I thought this was how I was supposed to dress!" I wailed. *Sheesh — if I'd known I was going to attract so much attention, I wouldn't have bothered hogging the bathroom all morning,* I thought.

Sighing, Lindsay hitched her swirl-patterned blue-and-purple backpack higher onto her shoulder. She was wearing dark denim jeans and a pink T-shirt with an elaborate picture of a Japanese tidal wave. Her hair flowed down her back in a sleek red curtain, and she had on mascara and pale pink lip gloss. She looked like she'd just come from a photo shoot for one of those teen clothes catalogs. Not typical Lindsay, but sweeter. "We're going for something between 'sweaty basketball jersey' and 'night on the town,' Nick."

"You said this dress was great!" I protested, peering at the mirror inside my locker.

"It *is* great!" Lindsay insisted. "But for school, you need something a little more casual. Like, you could wear the same outfit with Converse sneakers instead of flats, and maybe a jean jacket instead of that fancy one. And save the sparkly barrettes for evening. Oh, and ditch the handbag. And you don't need full makeup for school. Just some mascara and lip gloss ought to cover it."

"Thanks for telling me this *now,*" I griped, reaching for my barrette.

"What are you doing? Don't mess with it!" Lindsay said.

"I thought I was overdressed." This was getting way too complicated for me.

"You look great. If you start messing with it, you'll ruin the whole thing. Just go with this look today, and go more casual tomorrow," Lindsay advised.

Just then, Alex came storming up to us and yanked open the locker next to mine. "Thanks a lot, Nick," he spat, yanking off the tie he was wearing — pale blue with tiny sailboats. He actually looked very nice in a bright blue button-down shirt and khaki pants.

Lindsay and I looked at each other. "What did I do?" I asked.

"All the guys have been teasing me for wearing a tie!" my brother complained. He tossed the tie into the locker and slammed it. "You could have just *told* me that nothing special was going on today!"

"I tried!" I protested, but Alex had already taken off down the hall. I sighed. I was starting to think that it didn't matter *what* I said. The world was just spinning around me, regardless, making up its own reality.

The gym echoed with the sound of sneakers squeaking across the wood floor as Hannah bolted toward the basket. I limped up the side, trying not to jog too hard. One of my barrettes kept flopping against my scalp — it felt like it was about to fall out any minute.

"Open!" Carla shouted. Hannah passed the ball, but Anita grabbed it and darted the other way, sending everyone down court after her.

Sweat trickled down my cheek, and I swiped at it with my arm. *Oh, ew.* A smear of blush and concealer came off with the sweat. This really was *way* too much makeup. I ran my index fingers under my bottom lashes, hoping that my mascara wasn't leaking all over my face. That would be just perfect.

I hadn't seen Ben all day, but I thought I might catch him after practice. Maybe he'd drop by to see Hannah or something. And if he did, I didn't want to be looking like a complete mess. What was the point of spending all that time in the bathroom this morning if the object of my crushdom didn't even get a look at me in all my made-over glory? Besides, I wanted to try to make up for embarrassing myself the other day at the bar mitzvah. . . .

"Nick!" Anita shouted, passing the ball my way. She shot a rocket toward my left — it was a shot I would normally have grabbed easily, but I wasn't expecting it. The ball bounced into the bleachers.

"What was that?" Anita jammed her fists onto her hips as I chased the ball.

"Sorry!" I called just as Coach Chin blew her whistle. I grabbed the ball and came trotting back toward the team, who had gathered under the hoop.

The coach did not smile as I handed her the ball. "Sorry," I said again, wincing a little at her disapproving glare.

"Where's your head, Nick?" Coach Chin demanded.

I looked down at the floor and was nearly blinded by her brilliant white tennis shoes. Coach was right — my mind wasn't on practice. "I'm a little off today," I admitted.

"Yeah, Nick — for someone who wants people to pass to her, you were barely awake out there," Hannah chimed in.

Coach eyed her sharply. "Let me remind you that this is *team* ball," she said. She looked at the other players. "You all have to keep your heads in the game. You have to notice the other players and pay attention to what's happening on the court. Anita, that was a great steal."

Anita gave her usual lopsided grin as Ivy elbowed her in the ribs playfully.

That's what I love about Coach Chin — she was able to point out that Hannah's pass had been weak without even mentioning her name. It was the coach's way of reminding Hannah who was in charge.

"Nick, you're usually on the spot with the passes and free throws," Coach said to me. "We need you to play your strongest game."

I nodded. "I'll get it together," I promised.

Nodding, Coach read a few notes from her clipboard, then let us go five minutes early. "I want everyone here on time tomorrow," Coach said. "Our last game is on Thursday — it looks like half of the school will be turning out to watch us battle Westlake. I want us to play a tight game."

She wasn't kidding, either. The Booster Club had made huge banners advertising the game and had hung them all over school. GO GARFIELD BOBCATS! read the one in the front hall. It was a really cute poster, actually. Our mascot is a bobcat, but they had painted a cartoon cat gobbling up a pan of lasagna. DEVOUR WESTLAKE! it said underneath the cat.

"I can't wait to take on those Westlake girls," Carla said. "They think they're so great."

"They *are* great," Chi pointed out. "They've had the best record in the city three years running! They're undefeated."

"So *far*," Carla corrected as she turned toward the locker room.

"Yeah, but if Nick pulls her airhead act again on Thursday, we're dead," Hannah volunteered. She cast a blue-eyed glare in my direction, and I felt like an idiot. Hannah and Coach Chin were right. I had Makeover Brain, and it was affecting my game.

"Everyone has a bad day sometimes," Anita told her. There was a warning in her voice. "Lay off, Hannah."

Hannah shrugged, and the team trickled into the locker room.

"Coming, Nick?" Anita called.

"In a minute."

Anita let the door fall closed, and the team's chatter disappeared into the locker room. I picked up the ball that the coach had placed in a sack at the edge of the bleachers, then stepped up to the free throw line. I bounced it twice and let it fly.

Whoosh. Nothing but net.

I grabbed the rebound and stood at the line to take another shot. The clock on the wall over the door said it was three minutes until four. I wondered idly if Ben would come by.

Clang.

Bounced off the rim.

I chased the ball, shaking my head. I had to keep my head in the game, like Coach said. Still, I wondered if I was really being honest with myself. Here I was, shooting free throws. But why? Was it just because I needed the practice? Or was it because I was hoping for Ben to show up?

Well — couldn't I do two things at once?

I took a few more shots and made them all. Then I practiced my layups. I got lost in what I was doing and didn't realize what time it was until Hannah walked out of the locker room. "See you later, Nick," she called as she slipped through the gym door. Alone. I looked at the clock. Four thirty.

Ben had never even shown up.

Crud!

This whole day has been a total bust! I thought. All that worrying about my makeover and he never even saw me. And now it was four thirty and I had fifteen minutes to shower, change, and get over to Smoothie Queen to meet Lindsay.

I'll have to skip the shower, I realized. *Oh, ew — and I have to get back into my nice dress!* For some reason, that seemed even more revolting than slipping into a pair of jeans. Way more.

Great.

Didn't my brother say that guys like girls who smell nice? I would just have to pray that Ben didn't like smoothies.

DAY SIX

TUESDAY

Body Language! How to Find Out What He's Saying . . . When He's Not Saying Anything!

Interested guys will usually "mirror" your moves. They don't even realize they're doing it, but if you find Mr. Crushable tugging his ear at the same time you are, it might mean he likes you!

I ran my hand through my still-damp hair as I paced in front of the auditorium. Through the double doors, I could hear someone singing "Over the Rainbow" in a distinctly *American Superstar* audition-reject way. Rehearsal was running long this afternoon — long enough for me to get nervous. But at least I was feeling a little better about my outfit. I'd hurried to shower after practice and slipped back into the dark denim jeans, tunic, and oversized low-slung brown belt I'd had on all day. After my fashion overkill the day before, Lindsay had come over and scoped out my closet.

"Okay, Nick, the idea is to take it up a couple of notches from the usual," Lindsay said as she yanked a corduroy skirt from the rack. "Take it from a two to a six, not from a two to a ten."

"I'm going to ignore the fact that you keep referring to my clothes as a two," I told her.

Lindsay held up a pair of cutoff sweatpants. "Exhibit A." She tossed them in a pile we had designated: Too Ugly for This World.

"But won't that send Alex running for a tie?" I asked, pointing to the brown knee-length skirt she had in her hand.

"This? No — look, it's all how you wear it." She held it up to a turquoise long-sleeved T-shirt, then put a pair of flats beside it.

Okay — I would never have put turquoise and brown together. Ev-er. But it looked good. Very good.

"Keep the makeup and hair minimal, and you've got a look," Lindsay announced.

"Where did you learn how to do that?" I asked. "I thought you didn't know anything about clothes."

"Look, just because I used to *choose* to wear funky stuff doesn't mean that I can't work the prep look," Lindsay huffed. "I mean, when it comes to costuming, I'm a fast learner. And this is just a costume, right?"

I thought about that. Actually, Lindsay had a good point. This was just a costume. My Pretty Girl costume.

So, anyway, Lindsay spent the rest of the afternoon mixing and matching my wardrobe, so that by the time I woke up this morning, I had about a zillion casual-but-not-too-casual outfits to choose from. I looked good . . . but not so good that I freaked out my brother. Although he was still sulking about that tie incident the day before.

"Hey, Nick!" Appearing at the end of the hall, Greg gave me a huge smile as he trotted over. "Where've you been?"

"I've been around," I said vaguely, wondering why he was asking. Where did he think I'd been? Indonesia?

"Hey, I got you something," he said, digging around in his pocket.

"You did?" I was flabbergasted. *Jeez, I guess I made more of an impression at the bar mitzvah than I realized!*

After a moment, Greg came up with a bent ticket. "It's for our next wrestling meet," he said, holding it out to me.

"Oh." I tried to keep the disappointment out of my voice. He was trying to be nice, I could tell. But . . . wrestling? I wasn't exactly dying to go.

"Yeah, well, you seemed so interested in wrestling the other night, I figured you might like to come watch me pound a few guys into the mat!" Greg grinned.

He sure is cute, I thought. *But . . .*

"So, you'll come, right?" Greg asked. "We can go out afterwards."

No way, I thought. I couldn't imagine anything I wanted less than to go watch wrestling and then listen to Greg talk about *more* wrestling afterwards.

Then again . . .

Well, Greg is the Practice Guy, I thought. Suddenly, a piece of magazine advice ran through my head. "Say yes to everything!" the article advised. "You never know where you'll meet Mr. Right! Besides, sometimes things are unexpectedly fun. And — if not — they often make good stories to entertain your buds!"

Okay, at the very least, this will probably be a good story, I reasoned. *So — what the heck*? "Sure," I said at last.

"Great!" Greg pounded a fist into the flat of his hand. "We're really going to nail those Washington Junior High jerks!"

"I can't wait to watch that," I lied.

Greg sort of stood there for a minute, like he expected me to say something. I couldn't think of anything good, so I just asked, "Hey — are you coming to our game on Thursday?"

"Thursday?" He shook his head like he had no idea what I was talking about.

"The basketball game," I explained. *Wow — had he really missed the posters that were hanging all over school?* "It's the biggest match of the year!"

"Oh — that. You're on the team? Well, I hadn't planned to go, but . . ." Greg shrugged. "Maybe I'll come by."

I forced a smile. *Don't do me any favors,* I thought, but what I said was, "Great!"

"Okay, well, I'll see you later, Nick!" Greg gave me a little wave as he headed down the hall.

"Later," I called, tucking the ticket into the pocket of my jeans. All this boy-attracting stuff required a lot of *not* saying what's on your mind. Not exactly my strong suit. I preferred to *say* my sarcastic comments, rather than just think them.

I wondered how long I could keep it up.

I had to wait another fifteen minutes until Lindsay walked out — chatting with Ben. It's weird — I had expected him to be there, of course. I mean, I knew that he was on the tech crew and everything. But when I saw him in person, my brain kind of went on the fritz. *What is it about those chocolaty eyes that makes me go weak?* I wondered.

"Nick!" Lindsay said with a huge grin. "Ben and I were just talking about you!"

"You were?" I managed to ask, even though all I could think was: *chocolaty eyes chocolaty eyes chocolaty eyes. . . .*

"Yeah, about the big game on Thursday," Ben said with a smile.

"I was saying that we could play the hora, and you could fall over on the other team," Lindsay joked.

"Wouldn't that be an intentional foul?" Ben asked, the corners of his eyes crinkling.

That actually made me laugh. It's funny — if anyone but Ben and Lindsay had teased me about embarrassing myself, I probably would have wanted to die. But those guys were just joking around. And even I had to admit that whole bar mitzvah fiasco *was* really hilarious. Kind of. "Well, I don't plan on wearing heels on the basketball court."

"Good strategy," Ben shot back.

Dramarama kids dribbled out of the auditorium behind us as I wracked my brain for something to say. I thought about Lindsay's flash cards. *Have you read any good books lately?* It felt too school-related. *What kind of sports are you into?* Ben didn't seem to play any. *How do you know the host?* Totally off.

Okay, what do they say to do when you're not *talking?* I thought. I remembered reading something about mirroring — in other words, moving your body the way your crush moves his. It's supposed to send subconscious good vibes to your crush.

"So what time does the game start?" Ben asked, running his hand through his hair.

I ran my hand through my hair, too. "Three fifteen."

"We should get there right after the bell rings at three to get the best seats," Lindsay suggested. "Maybe we could all hang out together after you win." She wiggled her eyebrows at me, but Ben didn't notice.

"Ice cream?" I said, ignoring her suggestive eyebrows.

Ben cocked his head to the side, and I did the same. "I usually have to get home by five," he said. "But I could ask my mom."

"You'd probably be home by five thirty or six," I told him, checking my watch as he checked his.

Ben narrowed his eyes a little, then pursed his

lips, so I did the same. Then he held up his hand. I held up mine, moving my fingers as he moved his. A smiled curled at the edge of his lips, as I realized that he and I were giving each other the Vulcan salute from *Star Trek*.

"What are you doing?" Ben asked.

Crud! My mirroring moves were supposed to be subliminal! He wasn't supposed to notice them. I looked at Lindsay for help.

"Nick is just messing with you," Lindsay said quickly. "Aren't you, Nick?"

"Yeah . . ." I struggled to find a reason to be mocking Ben's movements. "It's just a crazy game I play with my brother sometimes," I fibbed.

Lindsay faked a laugh, and I faked one, too, and suddenly we were fake-laughing like my crazy puppet game was the best joke on earth. "Oh, yeah, Nick and Alex can play that game for hours!" Lindsay put in.

Ben smiled a little. "You two are nuts," he said, but he sounded like he thought we were funny, not certifiably insane, which was a relief.

Okay, change of strategy! I commanded myself, trying desperately to think of a question to ask him. Suddenly, I heard myself say, "So, Ben, if you could have any superpower in the world, what would it be?"

He took a minute to think that over, and I wracked my brain for another question. "I think I'd like to be able to read minds," he said at last. "I think it would be cool to know what other people are thinking. What about —"

"What's your favorite ice-cream flavor?" I asked, rushing on to the next question.

Lindsay rolled her eyes and huffed out a sigh. I flashed her a *What?* look. I mean, I was supposed to be asking questions, right?

"Uh, I like chocolate mint, usually," Ben said. His forehead wrinkled a little.

Okay! Getting answers! This is going great! "If you could take one thing with you to live on a desert island, what would it be?"

"Is this another weird game?" Ben asked, laughing.

I shrugged. "Just curious," I said.

"Ben!" called a voice, and my heart sank. Hannah was standing at the double doors that led into the school parking lot. She tossed her long blond hair. Wow — she'd actually blown it dry after practice. Now that's commitment. I'd just taken a shower and let mine air-dry . . .

. . . which meant that I was sporting the drowned rat look.

"Coming," Ben called. He smiled at me. "See you later, Nick. Bye, Lindsay."

"See you tomorrow!" Lindsay said. Then she shouted, "Bye, Hannah!"

Hannah ignored her and turned to walk out into the parking lot as Ben trotted after her.

"Bye," I mumbled. Once the door closed behind him, I turned to my best friend, whose arms were folded across her chest. "He's still with her," I pointed out, unnecessarily. "What am I doing wrong?"

"Nick!" Lindsay sounded exasperated. "What was with all the crazy questions?"

"I thought I was supposed to ask him questions!"

"Okay, but those were kind of high on the Random-O-Meter, don't you think?" Lindsay shot back. "I mean, why didn't you ask him if he had a good time at the bar mitzvah, or how the play was going?"

"Oh," I said, wincing. Hmm, those probably *would* have made more sense. "I don't think I was doing the mirroring thing right, either," I admitted.

Lindsay snorted. 'Nuff said.

"Do you think I blew it?"

My best friend took a deep breath. "Weirdly, I

think he thought the whole thing was kind of funny."

I glanced toward the parking lot, where cars were crawling by to pick up jocks, dramaramas, mathletes . . . everyone who stayed after school. Ben and Hannah had disappeared. "He left with her again," I said.

"I'm telling you, it doesn't mean anything," Lindsay insisted. "He likes you, I can tell."

Hope bloomed in my chest. I didn't know if it was even possible . . . but I wanted to believe it, anyway. "You really think so?"

Lindsay laughed a little, then linked her arm through mine. "I really do."

DAY SEVEN

WEDNESDAY

First Date DOs and DON'Ts!

DO: Beware of TMI! Too Much Information = Nothing Left to Say on Date Two. Try to listen even more than you talk.

DON'T: Keep an eye out for other cuties while you're out with your date! It's downright rude, and believe me — he'll notice!

"Check out my new bag," Lindsay said the next morning, holding out a black purse with yellow polka dots. It had a tiny yellow bow at the clasp.

"Super-cute," I told her as I shoved my math textbook into my locker and pulled out my social studies notebook. "Where did it come from?"

"I talked Mom into taking me to the mall after

dinner," Lindsay admitted. "Fuchsia Flower was having a sale."

"Hey, did you get the answer to number five on Ms. Ebersol's homework?" I asked, flipping through my binder. "I couldn't find it anywhere in the chapter." Our social studies teacher was famous for giving us trick questions. Sometimes the answers were located in the pictures or the captions instead of the text. Usually, she gave us extra credit if we could answer them all.

Lindsay turned pale. "We had social studies homework?"

"You missed it?" I asked. That wasn't like Lindsay. She always writes down her assignments in a little orange notebook with a pickle on the cover.

"Oh, crud!" Lindsay said, pulling her little notebook out of her bag and flipping it open. "I wrote it down — I guess I just spaced on it. Oh, man — I didn't do the math, either!"

"You can just do the math at lunch," I told her. "I'll help — it's easy."

"But social studies is a lost cause." Lindsay sighed, leaning against the locker next to mine. "There's two and a half minutes to the bell."

"It's not a big deal," I told her, which was the

truth. Ms. Ebersol lets you miss two assignments during the semester, and I knew that Lindsay hadn't missed any yet.

"Yeah — but it's weird to think that I wrote down the assignments and then forgot about them completely," Lindsay said.

I shrugged. "I guess you had Fuchsia Flower brain." I understood completely. This makeover stuff took up a lot of mental space.

"I guess so," she agreed.

Just then, someone tapped me on the right shoulder. I looked over, but nobody was there.

"Gotcha!" Greg said, appearing on my left. He winked at me, grinning. "So — I'll see ya later, right, Nick?"

"Oh — yeah!" I tried to sound enthusiastic, but I wasn't sure I succeeded.

"Why don't you bring Linda, too?" Greg suggested, lifting his eyebrows in Lindsay's direction. Then he swaggered away.

"My name is Lindsay," my best friend called after him.

"Lizzie — right!" Greg called over his shoulder.

"What was that all about?" Lindsay asked as the first bell rang. We fell into step toward homeroom, and I saw that Greg had stopped at his locker at the end of the hall. He had the door open, and was checking his hair in the mirror. I wasn't sure, but I thought I saw him wink at himself.

"He asked me to come to his wrestling match," I said. "Which I completely forgot about until this minute."

"Ooh, lucky you." Lindsay rolled her eyes.

"You'll come with me, right? It's this afternoon, at four thirty."

"Are you insane?" Lindsay demanded, pinning me with her hazel eyes. "I don't want to watch a bunch of sweaty guys beat each other up."

"Please," I begged. I knew that the magazines said that I should say yes to everything — but I just didn't think I could deal with going to the wrestling match by myself. Sometimes you just need backup.

"Forget it."

"Fine." I didn't want to bring out the heavy artillery, but it was looking like I had to. "Just don't ask me to come along the next time you want to see Angel Garcia in a musical."

"That was two years ago!" Lindsay cried.

"And what about the time you wanted me to go to the ballet because you heard Bobby Roberts would be there with his parents? Or the time we sat through three innings of baseball just to watch Joe

Anderson's pitching debut — at which he walked eight batters, I might add?"

Lindsay looked scandalized. "I bought you nachos at that game!"

"They were cold," I reminded her.

Lindsay groaned. "All right, all right," she said at last. "I owe you — it's true." Her lips curved into a frown, and she nudged me. I turned to look up the hall as Greg grabbed Sebastian Euks and put him into a headlock. "But then we'll be even." Greg glanced up from torturing Sebastian to give us a little wave.

"I'm okay!" Sebastian shouted.

I didn't really know what to do, so I waved back.

"He sure seems to want to impress you," Lindsay said as we walked into Mr. Moaksley's homeroom.

"Yeah," I agreed.

"Maybe this makeover *is* working a little too well," Lindsay said with a sigh.

"This isn't really *so* bad," Lindsay said as we sat in the bleachers later that day. The gym smelled of sweat and felt as though someone had turned up the heat to the "Valley of Death" setting. I'd just finished basketball practice in here a half hour ago, but it seemed like they'd increased the heat and the ick factor by about a thousand degrees. On the flip side, the Booster Club was selling sodas and fruit drinks, so we each grabbed one and were enjoying the view of the wrestling team members in their cute red uniforms.

"It's not really as violent as I thought it would be," I admitted, sipping my Mango Madness. My image of wrestling was based on what I'd seen on TV — giant guys in capes and spandex jumping on each other and stomping on heads. This was more like two guys crouching in front of each other while trying to boot the other out of a circle or pin his shoulders to the ground. Greg gave me a little wave as he stepped up to the mat. It wasn't hard to spot Lindsay and me in the crowd — there were only about fifteen other people in the bleachers. I waved back. "Greg made it sound like these guys were going to be pounding each other."

"Eh — he was exaggerating," Lindsay said just as Greg pounced on his opponent and slammed him against the mat.

A collective groan went up from the small crowd, and Greg looked up. He lifted one hand in what I took to be a *Let's hear a cheer!* gesture, and his opponent — a short guy built like a tank — took the opportunity to fling Greg away.

The two squared off again. This time, the Tank

grabbed Greg and hauled him off his feet. "Oh!" I cried.

But in the next moment, Greg brought his legs down and flipped the Tank over his shoulder. Then he jumped on him — he looked like a cat pouncing on a cricket — and pinned his shoulders to the mat. Match over.

The other fifteen people in the crowd went nuts as Greg stood up. "Who's the man?" he shouted. "Who is the *man*?!"

One of his teammates gave Greg a high five while another pounded him on the back. Meanwhile, poor Tank stood up and limped over toward the bench. I was busy feeling sorry for the guy when Greg peered at me and threw a wink my way. "Who's the man?!" he called.

"Do you think he really wants you to answer that?" Lindsay asked.

"He already seems to know the answer," I said through my clenched smile as Greg strutted back to the bench to sit with his team.

We had to sit through several more matches before the whole ordeal was over. Whenever someone on our team would throw or pin an opponent, Greg would let out an angry-sounding "Yeah!" and pump his fist in the air — like he was the one who had scored the point. The whole thing was pretty boring, but Lindsay and I amused ourselves by buying several more drinks from the Boosters and mixing the flavors. Mango-raspberry-banana was a winner, until we added in some Sprite. Then it just got weird.

"How did you like the tournament?" Greg said as he walked up to us. His blond hair was damp with sweat, and one of his blond curls was stuck to the side of his face. It was cute in a slightly disgusting way.

"Is it over?" Lindsay asked.

"I liked it," I lied. Well, it wasn't a complete lie. I'd liked sitting with Lindsay and counting the number of times Greg pumped his fist in the air. Twenty-eight, in case you were wondering.

"Yeah, we kicked those guys' butts. Can I have a sip of your drink?" Greg asked, grabbing our latest concoction from my hand. "I'm dying."

"Um — it's kind of —"

Too late — he'd already chugged it down. "Blech!" Greg frowned at the cup. "Man, this is *disgusting*. So — do you guys want to come out with us?" He gestured toward the rest of the team, who were busy pounding one another on the back and making their way to the locker room. "Matt knows a place where we can get chicken wings super-cheap, and we were going to have a contest to see who can eat the most."

Oh, gross. "I don't think we're really hungry. . . ." I looked at Lindsay, whose heavy-lidded look told me that payback went as far as wrestling, but not as far as chicken wings.

"You don't have to eat anything," Greg said. "You can just watch."

Wow — Greg really knew how to take an unappealing option and make it even *less* appealing. "Um, we actually have to — uh — study. . . ."

Greg folded his arms across his chest. "Is this some girl thing?" he asked. "Some hard-to-get game?"

Jeez! Can't this guy take a hint? "Greg, as hard as it is for you to believe, Lindsay and I really *can't* go," I told him. It took all my energy not to wring his neck, but I managed it. What restraint.

Greg pursed his lips. "Okay, whatever — play your little game," he said with a shrug. "Your loss." Then he turned and walked off.

I glanced over at my best friend, who was shaking her head as Greg slammed open the door to the locker room and disappeared inside. "I'm getting that he's not exactly dream date material," she said.

"That's putting it mildly," I agreed. Still, a pang

of regret stabbed me in the stomach. After all, wasn't I supposed to be testing out all my new flirting techniques? And I'd just offended Greg and let him go. . . . "Maybe I should have gone with him. What do you think?"

"Eh." Lindsay lifted a shoulder and let it drop. "Whatever. He was just for practice. Besides, you know *I* wasn't going to watch any wing-eating contest. Not for cash money. Not for a sack of gold."

"Yeah . . ."

"Don't worry about it." Lindsay clapped me on the back. "You've got to save your energy for the *real* guy."

"Only two more days until Hannah's party," I reminded her. "I need all the practice I can get."

DAY EIGHT

THURSDAY

QUIZ: Is He Mr. Right? Or Mr. Oh-So-Wrong?

He thinks the perfect gift for you is:

A. jewelry.

B. a romantic card and a teddy bear.

C. tix to a monster truck rally.

D. a wallet-sized photo of himself.

E. a dinner for two — that *you* make.

"Over here!" I shouted, waving like a frantic air-traffic controller trying to get the attention of a jumbo jet that's about to take off from the runway. Which, you might say, was what was happening at that moment. Because Hannah had possession of the ball, and it looked like she wasn't about to give it up, even though she was being double-teamed. "I'm open!"

"Hannah!" Anita called as she made a fast break down the paint, shaking off the twenty-foot Amazon who had been guarding her.

Hannah ignored her, of course. Ignoring us all, she lined up her shot and let fly —

Slam! Rejected!

The crowd went nuts shouting for defense as Westlake shot the ball down court in a matter of nanoseconds. A girl with a long black curly ponytail went in for the layup, nailing two easy points. Chi grabbed the rebound and passed it to the open player — Hannah, unfortunately.

Not this again, I thought as we made our way toward the basket. But, unbelievably, Hannah passed it my way, then pulled her famous little spin move and rolled off her Westlake guard. In a minute, Anita's Amazon was all over me.

Hearing someone scream my name, I looked up to the top of the bleachers. It was Lindsay. She was sitting with Alex — and *Ben*.

"Oof!" I tripped a little as the Amazon zipped away with the ball. She'd stolen it right out of my hands!

"What was that?" Carla shouted as I stumbled after the Amazon, who sent up a jump shot.

Swish — ouch.

I stood there, watching the net flutter. Thoughts

swirled and howled around me like the dust and debris in Dorothy's Kansas tornado — omigosh-how's-my-hair-my-makeup-is-running-I-don't-look-girly-right-now-crud-he-saw-that-steal-I-can't-believe-he-came-to-the-game-even-though-he-said-he-would-I'm-wearing-a-basketball-jersey-but-that's-because-I'm-on-the-team-does-that-make-it-okay? — and it took me a moment to realize that the game had moved on without me.

"Nick!". Carla shouted, and I lurched toward the basket, stumbling like Frankenstein's monster. The one good thing about standing there like an idiot was that nobody was defending me. Carla shot the ball in my direction, and I grabbed it.

"I'm open!" Hannah shouted.

Like I care, I thought, lining up my shot. I could feel the eyes of the crowd on me as I drove hard toward the basket.

Slap!

A tiny blond Tinkerbell–look-alike from the other team smacked the ball, sending it spinning toward the Amazon, who thundered down the court in the opposite direction.

Buzz!

Half over.

Stupid, I thought as I made my way toward the bench. *Stupid, stupid, stupid.*

"You'll still get 'em!" I heard Lindsay shout, followed by Alex's voice calling, "All right, Nick!" but I didn't look up to where they were sitting. I couldn't. I didn't want to risk meeting Ben's eyes — I was looking so sweaty and gross! And Hannah's hair wasn't even mussed. . . .

"This is not looking good," Anita said, eyeing the scoreboard. We were down by seven. That's not an easy number to recover from — particularly when the team you're facing is as good as Westlake.

"All right, everyone." Coach Chin gestured for us to gather. "This is our last game of the season. Let's keep our egos in check."

I looked down at the glossy floor, but I could feel her eyes on me. I should have passed to Hannah. I knew it. But I hadn't — because Ben was in the stands, and I wanted to score in front of him.

No — it's just because he took you by surprise, I thought. The stands had already been packed by the time the team came out of the locker room. It looked like the Boosters had done an amazing job turning out a huge crowd for our big game. And, even though I gave the throng a quick scan the minute I walked into the gym, I hadn't managed to spot Lindsay or Ben until moments ago. I hadn't seen Greg, either, for that matter — even though I'd personally invited him to the game. Not that I cared about that.

He probably ate too many chicken wings, I thought.

"We're here to win," the coach went on, "not to be stars. Let's play some team ball."

A bony elbow poked me in the ribs, and I looked up to see Hannah's blue eyes boring into mine. I knew what she was thinking — that *I* hadn't passed to *her.* That really burned me up — I actually felt like my toes were on fire.

"Take the game where we're strongest," Coach advised. "All in."

Everyone put a hand into the center. "Gooooo, Bobcats!" we shouted.

And, just like that, we plunged into the second half.

Right away, Anita took the tip and drove hard down the court. Stopping suddenly, she passed behind her back to Carla, who put the ball up toward the basket. Too wide — until Chi tipped it in. The stands exploded, the gym echoing with cheers.

Amazon grabbed the rebound, but when she stopped at the paint, I put a hand up and jumped. Anita grabbed the ball as it bounced off of my hand and passed to Hannah. Two more.

Suddenly, we were only down by three — but Westlake wasn't about to let us catch up. Tinkerbell flew down the court and landed a pretty jump shot for another three points. The crowd gasped and groaned.

Back and forth we went. Sweat was pouring into my eyes, blinding me, but I forced myself to focus on the game. *Don't think about Ben,* I commanded myself, which of course only made me imagine those chocolaty eyes glued to my moves.

Still, I managed a couple of sweet little passes, and sent in a couple of layups and a jump shot. I even made two more points on fouls. Hannah, meanwhile, was on *fire*. She was taking shots every chance she got, and a lot of them were going in.

Carla's main tactic seemed to be to force a foul every chance she got — she's great at shooting free throws — and Anita was grabbing rebounds like she thought she was playing for the WNBA. Chi was everywhere, stealing, spinning, blocking. And when Carla finally went down hard on her ankle on a personal foul, Ivy came in and started working her three-point shots. Things were really gelling for us in a way they hadn't in a while.

But if we were like a well-oiled machine, Westlake was like a high-performance engine. They were putting heavy pressure on us, matching us point for point. *If I weren't playing in this game,* I thought as I ran after Curly Ponytail, *I bet I'd really be enjoying it.* As it was, I felt like I'd just run the Chicago Marathon . . . and then run home to Denver from there. By the time the last ten seconds snuck up on us, I was pooped.

"Time!" Coach Chin called.

My knees wobbled as I made my way toward her. She held out her clipboard, studying our faces. I looked around at my teammates. They all looked about as tired as I felt.

"We can win this," Coach Chin announced, pronouncing her words slowly — letting them sink in. "But we have to want to. We're down by two with seven seconds on the clock. Someone's going to get at least two more points — it'll either be us, or it'll be them."

"It'll be us," I said firmly. I'm not even sure how I had enough breath to say that, but I did.

Coach Chin's dark eyes lingered on mine for a moment. Then she looked around at the rest of the team. "Well?" she asked. "Will it?"

"Yes!" the team chorused.

"Great," Coach said. "Here's the play." And she laid it out. Once the buzzer sounded, we would have possession. Anita would drive it up the line and pass to Ivy, who would send it my way.

“Let Nick drive hard to the basket,” Coach Chin said. “She’s good at moving people out of the way. Once we tie it up, we’ll look for a steal or block hard and hold on until overtime. All in.”

“Gooooo, Bobcats!”

My head was floating as I trotted back onto the floor. *This is my play,* I thought. *I’ve got to make it count.* I pictured myself making the basket. I visualized us going into overtime. “We can still win,” I whispered to myself.

Anita overheard my comment. “You bet your booty,” she said with a grin.

When the whistle blew, Anita took the ball and pounded up the line like a freight train. Amazon tried for a steal, but Anita was too strong. She threw a sharp no-look pass to Ivy, who pressed in toward the basket and sent a bouncer to me.

But Amazon had left Anita behind and was all over me. I turned my back on her and pressed in toward the basket as the clock ticked down. I’d used this move to pressure Alex about a thousand times, but Amazon was taller. *She’s going to block my shot,* I realized. *I can’t shoot over her.*

Four seconds. Three.

“Nick!” Hannah shouted. She was standing just outside the arc painted on the floor, being guarded by Tinkerbell. Tink was fast, but small. *Hannah can shoot it,* I realized. *It's still risky, but she's got a better shot than I do.*

And then a thought, like a bullet: *She'll get the glory.*

And then another: *Take the game to where you're strongest.*

And then another: *If the places were reversed, she'd never pass to you.*

Two seconds.

Another thought: *I'm not Hannah.*

I passed the ball.

It was as if everything was slow and enormous — I saw Hannah plant her toes just outside the line, then she pushed off, sailed into the air, lined up her shot, and it flew —

Swish!

Right through the net!

Three points clicked onto the scoreboard as the buzzer sounded. We'd just won the game! The stands went nuts as people mobbed the floor to hug and congratulate us.

"Hannah!" Anita shouted as she picked up Hannah and swung her around.

Normally, I think Hannah would have scowled at a move like that, but she was too busy whooping and laughing to mind.

"We did it!" Carla cried, wrapping an arm around

my shoulder. Then she let go and made her way to the blond heroine of the game. "Go, Hannah!"

Hannah grinned as Ivy wrapped her in a hug; then Carla joined in, then Chi, then the rest of the team.

"We did it!" Anita cried, hugging me.

She dragged me over to everyone else, and we jumped up and down in unison until I felt like I was on a trampoline or one of those space-bounce machines they have at carnivals. We were all laughing and whooping like mad.

"Hey."

I felt a hand on my shoulder and turned to see Alex standing behind me. "That was awesome," he said warmly, giving me a rare Alex hug. He has a special one-armed technique that is sort of half-hug, half-slap-on-the-back.

"Yeah?" I smiled at him, then felt myself blush when I realized that Lindsay and Ben were right behind him.

"You did it!" Lindsay crowed. "You beat the impossible team!"

"Well — Hannah saved us with that shot," I said.

"Sweet assist," Ben said enthusiastically, flashing me a huge smile.

He noticed my assist? I can't believe he noticed that! "Thanks," I said breathlessly.

“You really do have the moves, after all,” Ben said. He was wearing a red-and-blue-striped rugby shirt and oversized jeans, and a faint, familiar fabric-softener scent wafted up from his clothes.

“That was just so exciting!” Lindsay gushed. “I mean, I don’t really love sports, but that was probably the most thrilling game ever! I was jumping out of my seat half the time!”

“She really was,” Alex agreed.

I pushed my bangs out of my eyes and realized that my hair was completely wet. I suddenly became aware of just how sweaty and disgusting I must look. Like a half-melted slug. Nice.

But Ben didn’t seem to mind. He was still smiling at me with that Ben smile, making me feel like I was the one who scored the winning basket.

“Hey, where’s the party?” asked a voice, and in the next moment, Greg shoved his way through the crowd and appeared at my elbow. “Looks like you won,” he said. “Dang, we never get this many people at a wrestling match — what’s the big deal with basketball, huh?” He shook his head. “Sorry I’m late, but Matt bet me ten bucks that I couldn’t put him in a half nelson, so I had to prove him wrong.” He held up a ten-dollar bill and snapped it.

“Hey, Nick,” Lindsay said, completely ignoring

Greg. "Do you want to shower so we can head out for ice cream? Ben — are you coming?"

Ben jammed his fists into his oversized pockets. "Yeah — my mom said it was fine."

"Me, too." Alex grinned. "I told Mom to pick us up at the Big Moo."

"Sorry, guys, but Nick and I are about to head out to see *Ninja's Revenge,*" Greg announced.

"What?" Lindsay cried. "I thought we had plans!"

Ben's face fell, and I was just about to say, *No, no — this is a mistake!* when Hannah emerged from the crowd and locked an arm around Ben's. "Hey, there you are!" she said. "Come on — we're getting pizza!"

"We are?" Ben asked.

"Why, don't you like pizza anymore?" Hannah asked, blinking her blue eyes up at Ben. "I'll make them get that white pizza you're so nuts about."

All the breath blew out of me then, and my chest felt like a limp sail.

Ben hesitated, and his warm brown eyes flicked toward me. "Well, I —"

"Looks like ice cream isn't in the cards." Greg wrapped an arm around my shoulder.

By the time I shrugged it off, Ben was looking down at Hannah again. "Okay," he said at last.

"Great. See you, Nick!" Hannah called, dragging Ben away.

He craned his neck to look back at me, and I shouted, "Wait!" but my voice was swallowed up in the noisy gym. In the next moment, both Hannah and Ben had melted into the crowd.

"What happened?" Lindsay cried, her hazel eyes huge. "Nick!"

"Aren't we going for ice cream?" Alex asked.

"Let's head," Greg said to me. "I want to get good seats."

"Why don't *you* head?" I snapped at him.

Greg laughed a little. "What?"

"You don't get to just come in here and announce that we're going to a movie!" I shouted, poking him in the chest. "Especially not *Ninja's Revenge*! What makes you think that people are dying to go with you wherever you want?"

"Most girls *do* want to go wherever I want," Greg shot back. "This has never happened before!"

"Well, get used to it," I told him. "Because it's happening now." I felt hot tears press against my eyelids as I hurried toward the locker room. I just hoped I could make it before the waterworks started flowing. I wasn't sad so much as I was mad. Mad that I'd just missed my chance to hang out with Ben, mad that I'd "practiced" so much on Greg that he'd ruined my shot with the right guy, mad that I'd spent so much effort being a girly girl, and it was all wasted. Ben had left with Hannah. Hannah, who already knew what kind of pizza he liked. They were probably taking romantic bites off of the same slice, sipping from the same soda with two straws. That thought did make a tear spill over the edge of my lower lid. I swiped at it as it trickled down my face, mixing with the sweat from the game.

DAY NINE

FRIDAY

From Friend Boy to Boyfriend — Turn Your Pal into Prince Charming by This Weekend!

The next time he suggests hanging with a group, propose a one-on-one hang. Do something fun so that you can talk and remind him of the cool vibe between you! Check out an amusement park, take a hike, or fly a kite at the park. Give him a peek at fun, fabulous you, and he'll see you in a new light!

I stared down at the outfit on my bed: tan skirt, ribbed tee, red corduroy jacket, flats. I'd picked it out the night before. *Nice outfit,* I thought. *Someone would look really good in that.*

But I knew one thing — that someone wasn't going to be me. Not today.

I just couldn't bear it.

Lindsay had tried really hard to cheer me up after Ben walked off with Hannah the night before, but it hadn't worked. I'd lost. That much was clear.

And these clothes — well, they were just the proof that, no matter how hard I tried, Hannah would always be the real girly girl, and I'd always be the faker.

Forget it. I just don't have the energy anymore, I decided as I yanked open my dresser and pulled out my favorite jeans. Soft and worn, they had a familiar blue-ink star drawn on the knee and a tiny hole at the cuff. Ahhh. They felt familiar and as comfortable as a second skin when I pulled them on. I knew that Lindsay would want me to wear them with some kind of funky shoes and maybe a belted sweater. Instead, I pulled on a football jersey and a pair of bright green sneakers.

I ran a hand through my hair and grinned at myself in the mirror. *I know that girl,* I thought. *Hey, Nick — where have you been?*

Right here, my reflection said.

Whistling, I made my way downstairs to the kitchen, where Mom was bent over her newspaper and Dad was fussing with a toaster waffle. Alex looked up from his multicolored cereal. "Nice outfit," he said.

"Thanks." I slid into my chair and reached for the

granola. I don't know how Alex eats that stuff — it makes me fall asleep by second period.

Alex tipped back his chair and reached for the bright orange cereal box, pretending to try to find the hidden figures on the back. "I like that jersey," he said after a moment.

"Darn this thing," Dad said as he fiddled with the toaster. "I think it's broken."

"You gave it to me," I told Alex. As if he didn't know. As if we didn't both save up for Christmas, so that we could buy each other football jerseys to wear for the Superbowl. Go Broncos! Not that we made it to the Superbowl, but still.

"I know. I wasn't sure you wanted it anymore. I was thinking I might ask for it back."

I snorted at that. "Keep dreaming."

Alex grinned. "So," he said slowly, "does this mean that you and Lindsay are giving up the whole makeover routine?"

Mom looked up from her paper then. "Alex, eat your breakfast," she said. "Hugh, if you keep shaking that toaster, you really will break it."

"It's not toasting my waffle," Dad insisted, so Mom — with a heavy sigh — got up to help him out. This is their usual breakfast routine. My dad can cook an excellent dinner, but he can't handle the toaster.

"I'm getting kind of sick of looking nice every day," I told my brother. "I'm just not really sure it's worth it."

"That's a relief," Alex muttered, digging into his rainbow breakfast food. I could hear the cereal crunch under his grinding teeth.

"Seriously?" I asked, intrigued.

Alex scrunched up his mouth and rolled his eyes. "Definitely," he said. "Gimme a break. You two looked like you thought you were in some catalog."

I laughed a little, which made my hand wobble as I poured milk over my granola. "Well — that doesn't sound so bad."

"It's not *bad*," Alex insisted. "It's just not *you*. I mean — especially Lindsay. You know, she always dressed so different. And she has that cool hair. . . ."

"Cool hair?" I repeated. Since when had Alex noticed Lindsay's hair?

"Well, you know — she's been making it straight lately, but it used to be curly. And she used to wear it in crazy styles. I mean, she'd just do a little braid on either side and let the rest hang loose, and she'd look like some kind of . . . I don't know . . . mermaid or something. . . ." My brother caught me staring at him, and his ears turned red. "Well, she *did,*" he insisted. "And then you two started wearing those boring outfits and you looked just like everyone else."

My teeth clicked as I forced my jaw closed. *Whoa. What was* that *little monologue?* I wondered as I spooned up some granola. It was almost like Alex had a serious crush . . . on Lindsay.

Oh, my gosh, I thought. I mean, Alex and I had known Lindsay for so long, it had never even occurred to me that he could like her in *that* way. . . .

"And, you know, you're working your whole jock-girl thing," Alex added quickly.

"Alex, I think that Nick looks nice in everything she wears," my mother put in. "Here you go, sweetie," she added as the toaster popped up. She put the waffle on my father's plate.

"I don't know why it works for you and not me," Dad said with a sigh.

"Yeah, but this is her *personality.*" Alex pointed to my jersey, and my mother didn't argue. "Just like the funky hair is Lindsay's."

Lindsay again. Interesting.

"Kids, you've got two minutes," my dad said. "Better grab your books. I'm taking my waffle to go."

I abandoned the shallow lake of milk in my bowl and headed for the stairs to get my backpack. My brain was still whirling with what Alex had said. I didn't know what to make of the idea that my brother might have a thing for my friend. I wondered what Lindsay would have to say about it. She wasn't interested in him that way — I was sure she would have told me if she was. Poor Alex.

I guess everyone in my family was doomed to hopeless crushdom.

"I'm thinking we should go a little more dramatic with your eye shadow tomorrow night," Lindsay said as I sipped my raspberry-banana smoothie. "It's a party, it's evening, you can add some color. And a hint of liner on your top lids. Hey, do you have Charlie's chart?"

"Not on me," I told her. I didn't tell her that I'd tossed it into the garbage that morning.

"No problem, I remember most of what she said about your color family." Lindsay doodled a face in her notebook and started making notes in the margins.

My stomach sank. This morning, I'd hoped that Lindsay would see my football jersey and understand that I was done. Instead, she'd met me at my locker and said, "Nick, you're such a genius!"

"What?" I asked, surprised that I wasn't hearing from the Disapproval Committee about my clothes.

"To wear this hideous outfit one day before the party!" Lindsay grinned. "You'll look even hotter tomorrow night, by comparison. Like Cinderella!"

She'd been so excited that her pale skin glowed pink, and I just didn't have the heart to tell her the truth. *I'll work up to it slowly,* I'd told myself. And now we were sitting in Smoothie Queen, our favorite after-school place, and she was planning my clothes and makeup for Hannah's party — and I was *still* working up to telling her. Slowly.

"Okay, listen, I'm thinking you should wear the black skirt you wore to the bar mitzvah," Lindsay said now, marking it down in her notebook.

I hesitated. "I'm not sure —"

"You think the green dress?"

"I don't —"

"Nick," Lindsay said slowly, taking a deep breath, "I know what you're thinking. And I totally understand."

"You do?" *Oh, man. Thank goodness for best friends,* I thought. *It's so great that you don't have to explain yourself all the time —*

Lindsay pointed at me with her purple sparkly pen. "You're thinking that you don't want to look like you're trying too hard. But I'm telling you, Nick, you look great in that skirt and plenty of people will be dressed up, so don't sweat it."

Swallowing a groan, I took a sip of my smoothie instead. "Hmm."

"Tomorrow is the night to go for it," Lindsay chirped. "Ten days, and you're ready to really impress Ben!"

"Lindsay," I said, fanning my fingers against the bright red plastic table. "I have to tell you something — I don't want to go to that party." I cringed once the words were out of my mouth. I couldn't help it — Lindsay looked like I'd slapped her.

"What?" she breathed.

"Listen, it's over, okay? Face it — Ben left the game with Hannah. He doesn't want to talk to me."

She shook her head. "I don't think he —"

"Besides," I interrupted, "I'm sick of this whole routine. It takes me half an hour to plan an outfit, and another half an hour to do my makeup. This makeover is taking over my life! I mean, I just don't care enough to spend that much time on how I look."

"But you're getting really good at it," Lindsay protested. "We both are, right?"

"What's the point, though?" I shot back. "So I can attract a loser like Greg?"

Lindsay sat back in her chair, then reached for her blueberry smoothie. She looked really pretty today. Her long red hair was tied back in a simple low ponytail, and she had on a pale green T-shirt and a beige skirt.

I noticed that a girl at a table behind her had on the same shirt.

Suddenly, I felt like I understood exactly what my brother had been saying — with her crazy striped tights and funky hairdos, Lindsay always used to look like someone you wanted to talk to. Now she just looked like someone in the background on a teen TV show.

Putting down her blueberry smoothie, Lindsay said, "I know what you mean."

"You do?"

"It's a chore." Lindsay folded her arms and leaned against the brilliant red table. "It was fun at first, but now . . ."

". . . it's work," I finished for her.

"Yeah." Lindsay sighed.

"Anyway, I miss the way you used to dress," I told her. "Alex does, too. He went off this morning, talking about how you used to look so cool with your wild hair."

"He did?" Lindsay's eyebrows flew up, and her pink cheeks got a little pinker.

"I don't think I was supposed to tell you that,

but yeah, he did," I said. "So there are people in the world who like the real us. I mean — you know — even if those people are just Alex." I rolled my eyes.

But Lindsay was beaming. "He really said that? That he liked my hair?"

"He said that you looked like a mermaid when you wore it down." I drew an X over my heart with my finger, so that she would know I was telling the truth. "Anyhoo, so I don't want to get dressed up, and I really don't want to go to Hannah's party to watch her hang over Ben all night."

"I can't believe he likes my hair," Lindsay said, touching her ponytail. Then her hazel eyes snapped into focus. "Listen — I still really really really think you should go to this party."

"What? Why?"

"Because I think you're wrong about Ben!"

"Lindsay," I said as patiently as I could, "he always comes to pick up Hannah from practice. They hang out together all the time. They're practically a couple!"

"Practically is not totally," Lindsay said. "Besides, I just don't buy it. I've seen the way he looks at her, and I've seen the way he looks at you."

I shook my head.

"You're just nervous, but you don't need to be! Besides, isn't the whole basketball team going to be there? You should go just to celebrate your big win!"

"I don't know. . . ."

"Look, Nick . . ." Reaching out, Lindsay took my hand, giving my palm a squeeze. It's funny — I'm two inches taller than she is, but our hands are exactly the same size. "Please go to the party." Her eyes were pleading. "Just go and talk to Ben, okay? Go and have a good time."

"Why?" I asked. I wasn't saying no — I just really wanted to know why she seemed to care so much.

Lindsay shrugged. "Because you deserve to have fun."

"Okay," I said at last. "Okay, I will."

Lindsay beamed. "Great!"

"But wait — I'm not getting dressed up."

"But you *will* talk to Ben," Lindsay prompted.

"Yeah."

"Okay!" She leaned back, stirring her straw in her smoothie. "Okay, so — what *are* you going to wear?"

I thought for a moment. That was actually a good question. An image of Hannah at the mall popped into my mind. "Maybe I'll wear cleats," I said with an evil smile. "Just to make her mad."

Lindsay grinned. "Nick, I always said you were a genius."

DAY TEN

SATURDAY

QUIZ: Who Means More to You — Your BF or Your BFF?

It's Saturday, and that cutie you're eyeing asks you to see a movie. But you already have plans with your best bud! You say:

A. "Pick me up at eight!"

B. "Wanna go skating with me and my best gal pal? (If so, bring a cute friend!)"

C. "Are you nuts? I'm booked!"

D. "I'll get back to you after I text my BFF."

I can't do this, I thought as I stood on Hannah's front door step. *I can't just walk in there. This is crazy!*

Okay, here are all the reasons:

1. I don't even like Hannah.
2. I can't bear to see Ben hanging out with her.

3. Hannah's house is this really gorgeous, huge, fancy place, and I'm wearing a dumb, plain old T-shirt.
4. Hannah never wanted to invite me in the first place.
5. This whole girly girl experiment has been a disaster!

And just as I'd thought of 5 and decided that I had enough reasons to just tiptoe away from the brass lion's head with a knocker in its mouth, just at that very moment, someone reached around me and pressed the doorbell.

"Nick!" Carla said, flashing her trademark enormous grin. "You made it!"

"Yeah," I said as the door opened and a laughing Chi stood there with a very good-looking guy with wild, frizzy hair. Dance music drifted over me.

"Hey, Stefan!" Carla said. "Hey, Chi! Love that skirt! Lookin' good!"

Chi smiled and tucked her glossy black hair behind her ear shyly. She was looking pretty in a denim mini and a hot pink shirt with sequins. "You guys look great, too," she said, which was clearly a lie in my case, but was true in Carla's — she had on the red dress with black poodles that Lindsay and I had seen at Fuchsia Flower. It looked great with her black curls and sparkling black eyes.

"Thanks! Where's the nibbles?" Carla asked, giving me a little shove through the front door and into the brightly lit hall. "Nick and I are starving!"

Actually, I was just leaving, I thought, but I didn't say it because Chi shut the door behind us and said, "Everyone's kind of hanging out in the kitchen and the living room."

"There's food all over," Stefan added. "Hannah's dad is a chef, so —"

"I want some of that olive dip he makes," Carla said as we made our way down the red hall, hung with black-and-white prints. I just drifted along after them, thinking, *It's too late now. There's no escape. None.*

"I'm going back for more crab cakes," Stefan announced, and in the next minute, we were standing in a huge kitchen buzzing with girls from the team and from our class. Hannah was holding court at a stainless-steel kitchen island in the center. To my surprise, she gave me a little wave as I walked in.

"Hey, Nick!" Anita called from a spot over by the sink. "Over here!" Even super-jock Anita had on a sparkly silver shirt with her dark blue jeans. "Dip?" she asked, holding out a blue-and-white bowl. "Hannah's dad made it."

"Where is he?" I asked, mostly just to make conversation.

"Upstairs, hiding I think," Anita said, smiling. "He comes down every now and again to check on us, but I think he's feeling a little outnumbered."

I took a chip from the bag on the counter and swirled it in the creamy dip. *Mmm. Delicious!* I reached for another chip, but just as I took a bite, Hannah walked up to me and said, "Hey!"

Naturally, I dribbled dip directly onto my shirt.

"Great party," Anita said warmly. "And the food is awesome."

"Dad's the best," Hannah agreed, tossing her long blond hair. She had on a gorgeous blue print dress that really brought out the deep color of her eyes. I also liked the ice-blue eye shadow she had on.

For Hannah, wearing the Pretty Girl look wasn't just a costume. *It's her,* I thought. *No wonder Ben wants to hang out with her all the time.*

"Hey, Hannah," I said, swiping at my shirt with a red napkin. It didn't do any good, by the way.

"So, Nick, I wanted to say thanks." Hannah folded her arms across her chest.

"Thanks?" *For coming?* I wondered, not getting it.

"For the *assist,*" Hannah explained, like I was an

idiot. "We were both being guarded. You could have tried the shot yourself."

I shrugged. "You were more open than I was — your guard was smaller."

"Yeah." Hannah bit her lip, like she was thinking about that. "Well, it was a good move." And then she walked away.

"Wow — that's, like, the first time she's ever thanked anyone for an assist," Anita marveled.

"That was seriously weird," I agreed. But I had to admit — it made me like Hannah just the tiniest bit. It was nice to know that she could be human.

"Omigosh, the cuties, the cuties, the cuties!" Carla said as she joined us. She nibbled a crab cake, then put it back on her plate — which was piled with goodies — and looked around. "The cuties are everywhere! Ooh, there's Steve Carmichael — he's got the most adorable ears!"

"You're nuts, Carla," Anita said. She was smiling and shaking her head at Carla's boy-craziness.

"Look at Chi," Carla shot back. "She's been talking about Stefan all year, and there they are, sipping sodas in the corner! Oh, and there's Hannah's brother. He is just *so* cute!" She shoved the rest of her crab cake into her mouth.

"Hannah has a brother?" I asked, following her gaze . . .

. . . to Ben.

My mouth went dry.

"Ben Reynolds is Hannah's brother?" Anita sounded dubious. "They don't have the same last name."

"Okay, he's not her brother yet," Carla admitted, biting into a piece of bread slathered with cheese. "Buh he gwon buh," she said through her mouthful of food.

Anita and I looked at each other. "What?"

Carla held up a finger while she chewed. "He's going to be," she finished, once she had swallowed. "His mother is marrying Hannah's dad this summer. Didn't you guys know that? I thought everyone knew that! They're moving in here in a few weeks."

I stood there, gaping at Ben like a lunatic, thinking, *Brother, Hannah, few weeks, brother, not boyfriend, brother,* and all of a sudden, he looked up from the conversation he was having with Chris Angelo and smiled at me.

"Oooh, he's coming over!" Carla said. "He's looking at Nick! Come on, Anita, let's get out of here!"

"No," I said, my heart thudding madly. "Don't leave me!"

"Better take care of that dip on your shirt," Anita said as Carla gave me a little wave and my two friends took off.

"Crud!" Working fast, I turned toward the sink and ran my napkin under the tap. I scrubbed at the stain with my napkin, but only succeeded in getting red dye on my blue shirt.

"Looks like Drink-spilling Girl has returned," Ben joked as he walked up behind me.

"Hi!" I said brightly as I turned to face him. I looked around for help. Ivy was standing nearby, chatting with Josie and Marybeth, two other girls from the team. But none of them were looking my way. "Better stand a few feet away, or you may be next."

"I'll take my chances," Ben said with a smile.

Oh, this is just perfect, I thought. *Here I am, standing right in front of Ben wearing a rag with a stain on the front.* I wondered wildly if there was any way I could sneak into Hannah's room and borrow her makeup. . . .

"How was pizza the other day?" I asked.

"Delicious, as always." Ben reached for the bag of chips and held it out to me. "Have you been to Giovanni's?"

"That's my favorite place," I said as I took a chip.

"Mine, too — but don't tell Hannah's dad." Ben's eyes crinkled at the edges as he smiled. Then, suddenly, his face fell a little, and he looked around. "So — uh — where's Greg?"

"Who?"

The side of Ben's mouth twitched up into a smile. "That guy you went to see the ninja movie with? Where's he?"

"Probably at home, gazing at himself in the mirror," I said before I could stop myself.

Ben lifted his eyebrows. "I heard you two were going out."

"Oh, please," I said, grabbing another chip. "I could never go out with a guy who uses more beauty products than I do!"

Ben laughed. "That's good," he said.

A brief silence passed between us, and in that moment, I heard Carla's voice float over the crowd. I knew it was her voice, but she was doing an almost perfect imitation of Coach Chin. "Take the game to where you're strongest!" Carla cried, and several voices hooted in laughter.

The game.

I looked up into Ben's dark dreamy eyes, fringed with long lashes. I thought about how hard I'd worked at pretending to be a girly girl, just because that was what I thought he liked. I'd spent all that time on makeup and clothes and asking dumb questions, and the whole time, I had been playing to my weaknesses.

But what are my strengths? I wondered. Just

then, someone turned up the volume on the CD player.

"There's dancing in the living room, everybody!" Hannah shouted, leading the way. Half of the kitchen cleared out after her.

I looked up at Ben. "You're not going?"

"I'm not much of a dancer," he said. "Remember?"

Right — he'd said that at the bar mitzvah. "Me, neither."

"I know." Ben gave me a goofy grin, which made me laugh.

There was something about him — I wanted to go on talking to him forever. But now it was really too loud to have a decent conversation.

Take the game to where you're strongest, whispered a voice in my mind.

"So, do you want to go for a walk or something?" I suggested.

"Nick," Ben said, setting the bag of chips back on the counter, "I thought you'd never ask."

"It's actually kind of a romantic story," Ben said as we walked down the quiet street. Most of the houses in this part of town had old-fashioned streetlamps in front of them, and many of them were lit, so it was easy to see. A spring chill had crept into the air, so I huddled deeper into my jacket, but I wasn't cold as we walked toward Shepard Street, where there was a line of cute shops and restaurants. *This is a nice neighborhood,* I realized. It was only about two miles from my house, but I'd never been over here before.

"How did they meet?" I asked.

"They were high school sweethearts," Ben said. "Mom dated Antoine — that's Hannah's dad — when they were both seniors. Then they went away to college, and broke up and married other people. But things didn't work out between Mom and Dad."

"I'm sorry," I said softly.

"It's hard," Ben said with a shrug, "but they're still best friends, which is cool. I know a lot of people whose parents split up and they never spoke again. And it's better than Hannah's situation — her mother died three years ago."

"I didn't know." *Wow. No wonder Hannah is so moody,* I realized. *Her life isn't nearly as perfect as it looks.* "I couldn't imagine dealing with that."

"Me, neither." Ben shook his head.

We were both quiet for a moment. Finally, Ben took a breath and resumed his story. "Anyway, so our parents went to their high school reunion . . ."

". . . and ended up back together," I finished for him.

“Love at first sight.” Ben fiddled with the strings on the hood of his oversized sweatshirt. “Well — twenty years later. So that was last year, and the wedding is this summer.”

“That *is* a romantic story,” I said. A twig snapped under my green sneaker as we turned onto Shepard.

“And it’s cool, you know, because Hannah’s got a little sister, but I’ve never had anyone,” Ben went on. “Even though Hannah can be a pain sometimes, she can be really nice, too. And Lila — that’s Hannah’s sister — she’s the best.”

“You know what’s funny?” I said after a minute. “I actually thought that you were . . . going out with Hannah.”

“You did?” Ben stopped in his tracks and stared at me, then burst out laughing. “You *did*?” he repeated, then laughed harder.

“Well, I didn’t know!” I protested. “It’s not like you’ve got the same last name! And you seemed to spend all this time together. . . .”

“No, no.” He wiped at his eyes. “You’re right. I guess — I guess I can see why . . .” Then he started to laugh again, and so did I, and we hooted our way down the street for half a block. “Hey,” Ben said suddenly, stopping in front of a window. “Don’t we know those people?”

Looking up, I realized that the girl in the window — the one wearing the T-shirt with the sleeves ripped off over the thermal underwear top paired with torn jeans distinctly showing plaid tights underneath — was my best friend. And she wasn't alone. Lindsay and Alex were sitting at a table at the Dipper, laughing and sharing a banana split. I barely had time to think, *What the — ?* before Ben tugged on my sleeve and said, "Let's go say hi."

The bell over the door jingled and the sweet smell of hot fudge hit my nose as we walked into the pink-and-orange oasis that is the Dipper — the best ice-cream place in Denver. When Lindsay saw my face, she dropped her spoon.

"Hey, guys!" Ben said as we walked over to their table.

Alex looked like he wanted to hide under the table.

"We didn't plan this!" Lindsay insisted, her face turning pink. "I swear! I just happened to be online, and Alex IMed and said that he was bored, and I pointed out that we never got our ice cream the other night, so he said that we should try this new place —"

"Good idea." Ben nodded, somehow managing to ignore the fact that Lindsay was talking at warp speed. "So, mind if we join you?"

Alex looked from Ben to Lindsay, but avoided my eyes entirely. "Uh — no — uh —"

I smiled in spite of myself. Lindsay was blushing, and Alex was stammering. So they were crushing after all! And it was *mutual*!

"Um, have a seat." Lindsay gave me a guilty look as she patted the seat beside her.

Wow, she's got it bad, I realized. So the mystery boy Lindsay got made over for was, of all people, Alex. That was . . . weird.

But sweet.

Pulling off my jacket, I slid into the seat beside her. As Ben and Alex knocked fists, I leaned over and whispered, "You look great." My face was hidden behind her wild hair, so I don't think the guys heard me. She *did* look great. That crazy Lindsay outfit was a hundred times better than any of the pretty clothes she'd been sporting all week. A million times. Because she looked like *her.*

"I do?" Lindsay asked, smiling brightly. "You, too."

I looked down at the stain on my T-shirt. I was about to accuse her of being a terrible liar, but one glance at her beaming face told me that she really meant it. And who knows? Maybe I did look beautiful to her. "You're a good friend, Lindsay Sweet," I told her.

"And *you're* a good friend, Nicolette Spicer," she said back.

"Man, that looks amazing," Ben said, eyeing the banana split.

"It's killer." Alex spooned a mound of hot-fudge-covered vanilla into his mouth. "Mmmm. Don't you wish you had one? But you don't." He grinned madly, hot fudge blacking out half of his teeth. "Mmmmmmmmmmm!"

Lindsay laughed, shaking her head.

"Hey, Nick — you want to share one?" Ben lifted his eyebrows at me. "We can't let these guys have all the fun."

"Only if they make it with chocolate mint," I told him.

Ben grinned. "A girl after my own heart," he said.

"Ben," Lindsay said as she took a spoonful of whipped cream, "you don't know the half of it."

About the Author

Lisa Papademetriou's first hardcover novel, *Sixth-Grade Glommers, Norks, and Me*, was named a best book of the year by FamilyFun.com. Lisa is also the author of *The Wizard, the Witch, and Two Girls from Jersey* and the *New York Times* children's bestseller *Rani in the Mermaid Lagoon*, among other titles. She conducts writing workshops across the country for children and adults. To find out more about Lisa, please visit www.lisapapa.com.

check out

Miss Popularity

by Francesco Sedita

Another

Candy Apple book . . .

just for you.

CANDY APPLE

On the way home that afternoon, big Texas sunlight flooded the backseat of Mrs. Donaldson's minivan (the one with the bumper sticker that read: THE ONLY THING BIGGER THAN MY HAIR IS TEXAS). Cassie stretched her fingers apart, admiring the glint and glimmer of her favorite blue crystal ring and loathing the chip in her shimmering, shiny Blue by You nail polish. Blue — and if we're getting specific, teal — was Cassie's signature color. Oh, it was just so yummy! And it was the basis of Cassie's #1 Design Rule. *Teal: good. Teal and tons and tons of warm sunlight: um, delicious.*

"So, what are we doing this weekend?" Laura asked from the backseat.

Cassie turned around. "I heard that everyone's

going roller skating on Saturday for Donny McMahill's birthday."

"Really?" Erin asked, dreamily. She'd had a total crush on Donny since second grade.

"We should go. And maybe hit the mall first?" Cassie asked.

All the girls nodded.

"Erin, what are you going to wear?" Cassie asked.

Erin went white. "I have NO idea!"

"We'll figure it out. We have plenty of time," Cassie said, confident. "You can borrow my new flouncy denim skirt if you want. It would look SO cute on you!"

"Really? Thanks!" Erin said. "Because, really, Coke Zero is *not* my color."

The girls started to laugh again. Cassie was relieved Erin could joke about her spill.

"What's going on back there?" Mrs. Donaldson asked, her eyes in the rearview mirror.

Cassie leaned forward and said, "It's nothing, Mrs. D. Your beautiful daughter had a relatively un-beautiful moment today. But we handled it. She's still as beautiful as ever, right?"

Mrs. Donaldson smiled. "Of course!" She lightly bounced her hand against her hair-sprayed head.

They turned past Palace Boot Shop, where

Cassie got a new pair of cowboy boots each year for her birthday, and entered Houston Heights, Cassie's neighborhood.

Before she stepped out of the car, Cassie turned to the girls. "Okay, wrap-up calls in half an hour? Because we have some major homework to do. I can't believe it! It's like, welcome back from winter break, here's enough work to make you forget you had a vacation."

"Oh, please, Cass," Jen said, her copper-shadowed eyes twinkling in the sunlight, "you probably already did it all during free period."

Cassie grabbed her bag. "Thanks for the ride, Mrs. D!"

"Of course, sweetie. Tell your mom I'll call her later tonight."

"Will do!" Cassie looked at Erin, wanting to make sure her best friend was still okay after the unfortunate fall earlier. "How are we? Tell me before I go, so I don't have to start up CheerErinUp-dot-com when I get upstairs."

Erin laughed. "We are fine. Really. Thanks, Cass."

"It was funny. But so what? Funny is the best."

Erin smiled. Cassie reached over and gave her a hug.

Cassie blew kisses to the rest of the girls and

slid out of the car, her teal blue Candies clicking on the cement.

"I'm home!" Cassie called, the heavy door sighing open. She dropped her backpack and ran upstairs to her room.

She put her purse down on her desk, next to her blue rhinestone laptop. Design Rule #11 was obvious — basic, really. *Glitter, sparkles, and marabou make a perfect accent to anything.*

Cassie sat carefully on her bed, making sure she didn't upset her perfectly arranged pillow pile. She reached for her cordless phone to call a few of her other girls, to report on a *fab* pair of wedge heels she'd seen at the mall.

Just then, her mother called from downstairs. "Cassie, can you come to the kitchen, please?"

Cassie swung her feet onto the floor, slid on her marabou slippers, and walked to the mirror. She frowned at her frizzy mane, then sprayed hair spray with a flourish. Humidity in January was a real downer.

Her parents were at the kitchen table, papers spread in front of them. This wasn't a good sign. Cassie's parents only asked to speak with her like this when something was really up. Like when she was little little and her hamster, Peteykins, had gotten really sick.

Uh-oh.

"Hey, Cass, how's it going?" Her dad stood up and gave her a kiss on the head.

"Great." Cassie bit her lip. "Um, guys, what's going on?"

"We wanted to talk to you about my job," her dad said.

Oh no! Paul must've lost his job. (Cassie called her parents by their first names, Sheila and Paul. She had total respect for them — they ruled! — but "Mommy" and "Daddy" was just so, well, *7th Heaven.*) Cassie was ready to tell him that everything would be okay, that she would limit her clothes buying, and that she would do everything she could possibly do to help, even if that meant not getting manicures and pedicures every other week.

"Your father got a promotion, Cassie."

"That is so amazing!" Relieved, Cassie sprang out of her chair and hugged her dad.

"But it means that he has to move — we all have to move," her mom added.

Cassie plunked into her chair, her stomach sinking. *Move? To a new neighborhood?* "Where?" she asked.

"To Maine, honey," her mother said gently. "All the way up north."

Cassie looked from one parent to the other in shock. How could this be happening? Just a few minutes ago, her biggest issue had been frizzy hair, and whether or not to run for class president. And now — *now* — Cassie couldn't even process it. Her stomach turned and her heart began to pound. Leave Houston and all her friends? She was about to cry, she could feel it.

"I know this must be really scary and disappointing, Cass," her father said. "But it's going to be okay, you know?"

"I know," Cassie said, her voice trembling, a big wave of tears working its way through her. "But Maine? Really?"

Her dad laughed. "I know. It's far. And cold. But Maine is beautiful. And there's a great school that wants you to start as soon as you can."

A new school? Cassie hadn't even thought of *that* yet.